The Dangerous Dandy
The Ruthless Rake
The Bored Bridegroom
The Penniless Peer
The Cruel Count
The Castle of Fear
The Very Naughty Angel
Call of the Heart
The Frightened Bride
The Flame of Love
Say Yes, Samantha
As Eagles Fly
An Arrow of Love
A Gamble with Hearts
A Kiss for the King
A Frame of Dreams
Moon Over Eden
Fragrant Flower
The Golden Illusion
No Time for Love
The Husband Hunters
The Slaves of Love
The Ghost Who Fell in Love
Passions in the Sand
An Angel in Hell
The Incredible Honeymoon
The Dream and the Glory
Conquered by Love
Love Locked In
The Magic of Love
The Taming of Lady Lorinda
The Wild Cry of Love
Kiss in the Moonlight
The Marquis Who Hated Women
A Rhapsody of Love
Look, Listen and Love
The Wild, Unwilling Wife
The Curse of the Clan
Gypsy Magic
Fire in the Blood
White Lilac
The Outrageous Lady
The Passion and the Flower
Love, Lords and Lady-birds
The Hell-cat and the King
The Sign of Love
The Castle Made for Love
A Fugitive from Love

A Runaway Star
A Princess in Distress
Flowers for the God of Love
Lovers in Paradise
The Drums of Love
The Prince and the Pekingese
A Serpent of Satan
Imperial Splendour
Light of the Moon
The Duchess Disappeared
Terror in the Sun
Women Have Hearts
A Gentleman in Love
The Power and the Prince
Free from Fear
A Song of Love
Little White Doves of Love
Lost Laughter
Punished with Love
The Prude and the Prodigal
The Goddess and the Gaiety Girl
The Horizons of Love
The Waltz of the Hearts
Dreams Do Come True
A Night of Gaiety
The River of Love
Gift of the Gods
Love at the Helm
An Innocent in Russia
Love Wins
The Wings of Ecstasy
Tempted to Love
Love on the Wind
Moments of Love
Lucky in Love
Music From the Heart
A King in Love
Winged Victory
Love and the Marquis
Love and Lucia
A Duke in Danger
Love is Heaven
A Very Unusual Wife
Love With Love
Love Comes West
Temptation for a Teacher
Alone and Afraid
A Victory for Love

BARBARA CARTLAND

LOOK WITH LOVE

Pan Original
Pan Books London and Sydney

First published 1985 by Pan Books Ltd,
Cavaye Place, London SW10 9PG
9 8 7 6 5 4 3 2 1
© Cartland Promotions 1985
ISBN 0 330 28810 5
Photoset by Parker Typesetting Service, Leicester
Printed and bound in Great Britain by
Cox & Wyman Ltd, Reading

Barbara Cartland's Experience on Health

1930–2
Studied herbal medicine with the famous Mrs Lyell of Culpepper.

1931–3
A patient and a student of Dr Dengker of Baden-Baden. First use of olive oil as an internal treatment of liver complaints, colitus and inflamation of the bowel.

1930–7
Helped Lady Rhys Williams giving vitamin B to treat habitual abortion and malnutrition in distressed areas.

Studied the first use of vitamin E with brood mares and later for barren women.

1935 onwards
Worked with Dr Pierre Lansel, MD, first practioner in England to give injections of vitamin B and C. Followed his experiments with hormones for rejuvenation and the Nieheims treatment of cell therapy. Studied with two eminent doctors the effect of oil injection on external haemorrhoids.

Studied the nutritional condition in her brother's Parliamentary Constituency, King's Norton Division of Birmingham, where there was malnutrition owing to low wages.

Practised Yoga exercises and breathing with the only white Yogi in the world. Wrote in a monthly magazine on the subject.

Studied nutrition in Montreal and did two lecture tours in lower Canada during which visited a large number of schools and hospitals.

1939–45

County Cadet Officer for the St John Ambulance Brigade, Bedfordshire. Arranged first aid and home nursing lectures and discussed nutrition with doctors from overseas. Only Honorary Member of the Officers' Mess (Doctors and Psychiatrists) of 101 Convalescent Home, the largest Rehabilitation Centre in Great Britain.

Looked after 10,000 RAF and the US Flying Fortresses until the American Red Cross arrived.

Studied nutrition of the troops and the conditions in the Prisoner of War camps.

As Lady County Welfare Officer of Bedfordshire Voluntary Junior Commander (Captain) ATS, dealt with innumerable complaints about food from RAF camps, Secret Stations and Searchlight Posts and with the health and employment of pregnant mothers from all three Services. Studied conditions in the hospitals treating the women in the armed Services.

1945

Was introduced in America to the first B-Complex Multi-Vitamin (synthetic) capsule. On return home was closely in touch with the American manufacturers of vitamins, receiving regular reports, literature and supplies until the Organic Vitamin Company opened at Hemel Hempstead.

1950

Vitamins saved her life. Kept fifty-two farrowing sows on her farm in Hertfordshire and experimented by giving them and the boars brewers yeast from a brewery. For four years they held the record production for Great Britain with an average of eleven a litter. Method copied by Sir Harry Haig for Ovaltine. Her prize-winning bull was given vitamin E injections.

1955
Published: *Marriage for Moderns*, *Be Vivid Be Vital*, *Love, Life and Sex*, *Vitamins for Vitality*, etc.
Began her lectures on health.

Became a County Councillor of Hertfordshire, on Education and Health Committees for nine years.

Studied nutrition with regard to school meals. Deeply concerned with the health and conditions of old people. Was so horrified at the way they were fed in some homes, and their general treatment, that her daughter, then Viscountess Lewisham, visited 250 homes all over Great Britain.

Following her reports and Barbara Cartland's and the tremendous press publicity involved, the Minister for Housing and Local Government (The Rt. Hon. Duncan Sandys, M.P.) instigated an enquiry into the 'Housing and Conditions of the Elderly'.

Was on the Managerial Committee of several old peoples homes and a Patron of Cell Barnes, the largest home for retarded children in Great Britain.

Visited and inspected innumerable hospitals, clinics and homes for the elderly and for children. Started her fight for better salaries and conditions for midwives and nurses, which brought her into close contact with many of the teaching hospitals and Royal College of Midwives.

1958
Was host to Professor Ana Aslan, founder of H3, on her first visit to England at the invitation of 400 doctors. Also tried acupuncture and the Cryiac Method of holding a slipped rib or disc.

1960
Started to write monthly for *Here's Health*.

Co-founder of the National Association for Health.

Answered 5,000 letters a year – 10,000 in 1984. *The Magic of Honey* (1 million copies), doubled the sale of honey in Great Britain and over the world.

Lectured on health to:

The Southgate Technical College
The Queen Elizabeth College of Nutrition
The Polytechnic
The Hertfordshire Police Cadets
Two lectures in the Birmingham Town Hall to audiences
  of 2,500
Frequent lectures to Midwives, Universities, Rotary
  Clubs, etc.

1964–1978
Given a Civic Reception by the Mayor of Vienna for her work in the Health Movement.

Had private discussions on health, herbs and health foods with:

The Ministers of Health and Sciences in Mexico, Japan and India. Professors and scientists in Mysore working on the development of agriculture in the famine areas near Kerala with the India Ladies Committee and officials on health in Bombay, New Delhi and Mysore.

In touch with the Indian Guild of Service working among orphans, and in the poor areas in India, and saw the conditions among the first three million Pakistanis who moved into Calcutta in 1958.

Visited the new refugee areas in Hong Kong, was the first woman to visit (with the police) the Chinese border, seeing the conditions of the workers.

Visited Nepal and saw the insanitary conditions in Katmandu and the rat-infested refuse in the streets. Discussed the conditions with officials.

Visited hospitals, clinics and old people's homes in many parts of India, Bangkok, Hong Kong, Singapore, Switzerland, Austria and France.

Taken on a special visit with five doctors and scientists to inspect the Vitel Clinic in France.

Visited the slums of Delhi, Calcutta, Bombay, Phnom-Penh (Cambodia), Taiwan, Singapore, Rio, Harlem (New York), Glasgow, London, and had talks with the leading doctor in Istanbul and shown clinical trials undertaken.

Is closely in touch with the pioneers of the Health Movement in South Africa.

Invited – as a guest – to Yugoslavia, Germany and France.

1978
Visited Leningrad and Moscow and had talks with the scientists on old age problems and the use of Ginseng.

1984
A Dame of Grace of St John of Jerusalem; Chairman of the St John Council, and Deputy President of the St John Ambulance Brigade in Hertfordshire. One of the first women in 1,000 years to be on the Chapter General; President of the Hertfordshire Branch of the Royal College of Midwives; President of the National Association for Health.

Author's note

In this busy mechanical age we often forget that the faith of primitive people has since the beginning of time set an example for mankind.

Anyone who has lived amongst the natives in Africa, India, or in other isolated parts of the world, has realised that they can effect what seem to us miracles, by thought and by faith in themselves and their Gods.

Even a witch doctor cannot prevent an African from dying, if he has made up his mind to do so, and the Voodoo of South America has many strange things it could teach those who despise it, if they would trouble to listen.

Soldiers who served in India during the days of the Raj can tell tales of Indians who knew when one of their close relatives died three hundred miles away, long before it was possible for them to receive any physical communication of the death.

What these people use is their instinct, or what the Egyptians called their 'Third Eye', which we today have discarded for written references, certificates and documents of every sort.

So much of what is called 'clairvoyance' is merely the person in question using the instinct which was given to all of us and which can be, if we use it properly, both a protection and an inspiration.

Chapter One
1886

As the train steamed into Victoria Station Ilita had a sudden impulse to cling to Sister Angelica.

Even as she thought of it she knew she was being ridiculous. At the Convent she had never liked Sister Angelica who had been in charge of the laundry and taught the girls the more boring types of sewing which included darning and mending.

But now her lined face and bespectacled eyes seemed all that was familiar, while ahead there was only apprehension and the emptiness of the unknown.

"If only Papa was here, it would be wonderful to be back in England," Ilita told herself and felt the pain that, even after a year and a half, invariably accompanied thoughts of her father.

Then her travelling companion, daughter of the Italian Ambassador at the Court of St. James's, was standing up at the window crying:

"I can see Mama! She is standing on the platform. Oh, Sister Angelica, please let down the window!"

"All in good time, my child," Sister Angelica replied. "If your mother has come to meet you, then you can be quite certain she will find you."

The Italian girl did not listen, and Ilita wondered if there would be anyone to meet her except perhaps a senior servant.

It seemed impossible that on her return home to England the only relative she was certain of seeing was an Aunt whom she had only met once before in her life and who she had thought then did not like either her or her father.

"Perhaps she will be pleased to see me now," she told herself and tried to find it a consoling thought, though her instinct was certain it was something which was very unlikely.

All the time the train had been carrying her from Florence to England, Ilita, looking back on all that had happened, had tried to imagine how things might have worked out very differently.

She might now, if fate had not struck in a devastatingly cruel manner, have been going to Darrington Park to be with her father.

Instead of which her father was dead and so, although it seemed incredible, was his younger brother, who had succeeded him as the sixth Earl.

Now there was only a young boy still at school to carry on the family tradition.

Ilita knew that never had it crossed her father's mind at any time that he might inherit the huge house in Buckinghamshire and the Earldom of which the family had always been extremely proud.

As a second son, with a father who was still a youngish man and a brother two years older than himself, Marcus Darrington-Coombe decided that with the small income, which was all his father allowed him, he would explore the world.

He had married a girl who was as adventurous as he was, and together they climbed mountains, visited unmapped parts of Asia, sailed up crocodile-infested rivers, and crossed uncharted deserts with the optimism of amateur explorers who found nothing impossible.

When Ilita was born, she did not inhibit their journeys, she merely went with them.

She was rocked asleep in a basket on the back of a camel, carried up mountainsides in a pannier attached to a Yak, and learnt to exist on strange foods which might have killed other children.

They had little money but everything was fun, and Ilita could remember her childhood seemed always to be radiant with laughter and love.

Then three years ago, when she was fifteen years old, disaster struck.

Coming back by sea from a journey in Africa, they had landed in Naples and both her father and mother were stricken down with a strange fever which the doctors did not recognise and had no idea how to cure.

When her mother died quickly, almost before they realised how ill she was, her husband and her daughter found it impossible to believe that life could go on without her.

It was actually Ilita who had the stronger will of the two. She forced her father to eat and gradually made him interested in things that were going on around them – excavations in Pompeii, the discovery of a Roman Villa on Capri – and when at last he made an effort for her sake, he gradually became a little more normal.

For some months he was weak from the fever that had killed his wife and it was then that unexpectedly Ilita's godmother, Mrs. Van Holden, had appeared.

She had been a close friend of her mother's and hearing they were in Naples had come from Rome where she was then staying, to tell them how desperately sorry she was at their bereavement.

"I loved Elizabeth," she said with tears in her eyes, "and although we saw very little of each other after I married an American, I cannot bear to think that she is no longer in the world which she made beautiful because she lived in it."

As she sat with Ilita and her father in the untidy garden of the cheap hotel in which they had installed themselves, she talked of the days when she and Elizabeth, who had been the same age, had made their curtsies at Buckingham Palace and thought they would conquer the world because they were so young and happy.

"And you know what happened?" Mrs. Holden asked Ilita with a smile. "Your grandmother was quite certain that your mother would make a brilliant marriage because she was so beautiful. I used to laugh and say she had every Prince, Duke and Marquis in the English aristocracy lined up for her!"

Knowing the answer, Ilita asked:

"What happened, Godmama?"

"She saw your father at a Ball," Mrs. Van Holden replied, "and fell in love! After that, if every King, even the Shah of Persia himself, had fallen on their knees in front of her, she would not even have known they were there!"

"And I fell no less in love with her! She was the most beautiful thing I had ever seen in my life," Ilita's father said, and she could hear the pain in his voice.

"And I, too, fell in love," Mrs. Van Holden said, as if she did not wish to linger on thoughts that would make them unhappy. "But my family were horrified because he was an American! He was an Attache at the American Embassy in London, and after we married we went back to America together. I can honestly say I have been a very lucky and happy woman."

There was a little pause before she added:

"Unfortunately I was not blessed as your mother was by having any children."

"I am sorry about that," Ilita's father said.

"So am I," Mrs. Van Holden answered, "and that is why I am going to talk to you very seriously, Marcus, about my goddaughter."

Ilita looked wide-eyed at Mrs. Van Holden as she went on.

"I suppose you realise she is going to be as beautiful as her mother! So it is very important that before she makes her début in England she should go to a Finishing School."

"I do not know what you are saying!" Ilita's father exclaimed in a bewildered tone. "I have never visualised Ilita as a conventional débutante."

"Then it is very selfish of you not to!" Mrs. Van Holden said. "Of course Ilita must have her chance as Elizabeth and I had ours."

She sighed before she continued:

"Although she may turn her back on the Balls, the Receptions and the glamour of London Society which is more grand than anywhere else in the world, she must at least have the choice of knowing what sort of life she would prefer in the future."

"I want to be with Papa!" Ilita said quickly.

"And I want my daughter with me," her father added, putting his arm around her shoulders.

"You have had her for nearly sixteen years," Mrs. Van Holden said, "and now, my dear man, you have to think of her not as a child but as a young woman who one day will be a wife and mother."

Ilita felt her father's arm tighten protectively around her shoulders and she knew from the expression in his eyes that the ideas that Mrs. Van Holden had proposed had never occured to him before.

They talked and argued about Ilita's future all that afternoon and the discussion continued when they dined with Mrs. Van Holden at the largest and most expensive hotel in Naples where she was staying.

Although she had travelled so much with her father, Ilita had seldom seen the inside of the luxury hotels which they could not afford, and was actually far more at home in a tent hurriedly erected in an oasis or a dak bungalow in some obscure Indian village.

She was acutely concerned that compared with Mrs. Van Holden and the other diners in the restaurant she was extremely badly dressed, and even her father, handsome though he was, seemed somehow ill at ease in his evening clothes compared to the other gentlemen around him.

"I have been thinking things over, Marcus," Mrs. Van Holden said as dinner finished, "and what I have decided is that my present to my goddaughter, which is somewhat overdue as I had no idea where in the world you might be on her last two birthdays or even at Christmas, will be fifteen months' education in the most renowned and important Convent School in Florence."

Ilita gave an almost audible gasp as her godmother went on:

"I have made enquiries from the American Ambassador and one or two distinguished Italians, and they all tell me that the Convent of St. Sophia, which is both a school

15

as well as an enclosed Order, is the smartest and the most important in the whole of Europe."

"Oh, please," Ilita cried, "I do not want to go to school!"

"A sentiment that makes me quite sure it is something you should do," Mrs. Van Holden replied.

Her voice sounded a little harsh, but she smiled as she said:

"I know being with your beloved mother who was very intelligent and very well read, was an education in itself, and of course it would be impossible travelling as you have with your father not to learn languages."

She paused.

"But there are other things a young lady of fashion should know, and that is exactly why the young girls of the aristocracy, whether they are Italian, French or English, have usually a year at Finishing School before they emerge like butterflies on an astonished world."

Ilita had laughed, thinking this way of putting things was funny, but her godmother went on:

"I promise you, dearest child, you will be a very beautiful, much acclaimed butterfly when you do appear. And since your dear mother will not be able to present you at Buckingham Palace, I will come over from America to do so and will arrange that you are sponsored, if not by one of your relations, by one of mine, and I will give the finest and most exciting Ball for you that London has ever seen!"

Feeling somewhat frightened by what she was hearing, Ilita slipped her hand in her father's under the table, silently begging him not to agree.

But she had known before he spoke that because he loved her he recognised that Mrs. Van Holden was speaking sense and that it was, if she thought about it, what her mother would have wanted for her.

After that, Ilita thought, everything happened so quickly she did not have time to think.

Before she could realise what was happening she found herself in the Convent in Florence, possessing a whole outfit of new clothes her godmother had bought for her, and although she tried to cling to him, her father disappeared.

"Where are you going, Papa?" she had asked.

"I have an invitation to investigate some new excavations in Turkey."

"Oh, Papa, let me come with you," Ilita begged.

"We will go away later when you are free to do so," he promised.

"But you will not go without saying goodbye to me?"

"No, of course not," he replied. "It is going to take me a month or more to get everything ready and I will come to Florence before I leave. Of course, I will tell you exactly where I am going so that you can get in touch should anything happen."

Ilita wanted to say that nothing was going to happen to her, but it would be agony to know that he was going to be so far away from her.

She was well aware that when he was on an exploring trip it was often almost impossible for him to communicate with the outside world.

But when he had come to see her just before leaving for Turkey, he had very different news for her from what she expected.

She had known the moment she saw him that something was wrong from the expression on his face and because she knew his every mood and every vibration that came from him. Before he even spoke, she said, as she put her arms around him:

"What is the matter, Papa? What is wrong?"

"Who said anything was wrong?" her father enquired.

"I know it is. I can feel it."

"There is nothing exactly wrong," her father said, sitting down on the hard, uncomfortable sofa in Mother Superior's sitting room.

"Then why are you worried?"

Her father smiled at her and it illuminated his face, making him look even more handsome than he did already.

17

"You always know what I am feeling, just as your mother did," he said. "Yes, I am worried because something very unexpected has happened and I have to make up my mind today whether I go on this trip that I have planned or go back to England."

"To England, Papa?"

Her father nodded.

"I learnt this morning from a messenger, who had been especially sent from England to find me, that your grandfather died a week ago."

Ilita listened wide-eyed.

Although she could barely remember her grandfather, whom she had not seen for some years, her father had often talked about him, and she knew he had ardently disapproved of what he thought was his son's wasteful, unproductive way of living.

"Are you very upset that your father is dead, Papa?" she asked.

"I never thought of his dying," her father replied. "After all, he was little over sixty and always seemed so strong and I suppose indestructible is the word I should use."

"And you think you ought to go back for the funeral?"

"The funeral is over," her father answered. "They could not find me in time to tell me about it. But I am now the Earl of Darrington."

Ilita stared at him in amazement before she said:

"But . . your brother . . Uncle Lionel?"

"He was killed in the Sudan nine months ago. It must have happened when we were beyond the reach, as we so often were, of the newspapers, and until this morning I had no idea that he was not alive and with his Regiment."

Realising that her father was upset, Ilita laid her hand on his.

"I am sorry, Papa."

"So am I, desperately sorry, because he would have made an excellent head of the family and a far better peer than I am ever likely to be."

Ilita had laughed.

"That is untrue, Papa. I remember Mama saying the only thing she ever regretted was that she would not see you wearing a coronet and that you would be far better looking than anyone else in the House of Lords."

Her father had laughed at that and had said:

"The truth is, Ilita, I am not cut out for the pomp and ceremony of being an English aristocrat. I should feel constricted even in the huge rooms of Darrington, while the broad acres surrounding it would make me long for distant horizons and the snowy peaks of unconquered mountains."

Before Ilita could answer he went on:

"I know exactly what everyone will say, that it is my duty, my responsibility, and the type of life to which God has been pleased to call me. All right! All right! I accept all that!"

His voice had sharpened as he went on:

"But I am damned if I will give up what will be my last and perhaps my most exciting journey before I become a pillar of respectability and undoubtedly a pompous bore!"

Ilita's laughter had rung out and despite himself, the irritation vanished from her father's eyes and he laughed too.

"You are quite right, my darling. You are thinking that I am being over-dramatic, which is exactly what I am!"

He got up from the sofa to walk about the austere room, its only decoration being a crucifix over the desk where the Mother Superior wrote.

For a moment he did not speak and Ilita said pleadingly:

"Please, Papa, take me with you. I know you intend to go on your expedition to Turkey as planned, and it would be so wonderful if we could be togther!"

Her father looked at her and she knew he was tempted.

"It is what I would enjoy more than anything in the world," he said, "but, my precious, I know your god-mother was right when she insisted that I sent you here. Just as I shall have to do my duty in the future, you must do yours."

"I will try, Papa, I promise," Ilita said. "Only if you can play truant, so can I."

"Not so easily," her father replied, "and you know that giving up six months more of your education would be a mistake. What I will promise," he said, "is that when you finish here at the Convent, before you become the society butterfly that your godmother is planning, you and I will go off somewhere alone where no one will find us and we will discover something so exciting, so different that the whole world will acclaim us!"

"I only want to be with you, Papa."

"That is what I want too," her father said. "We will start on our exploration the very moment they give you all the prizes and send you away from here as the brightest and most intelligent pupil they have ever had."

Ilita laughed, but at the same time she knew with a sinking of her heart that her father would be going to Turkey without her.

That night when he had left, as she was to do for a dozen nights after, she cried herself to sleep.

It was no consolation to learn that now she was Lady Ilita Darrington-Coombe and of far more consequence in the eyes of her school-mates than she had been previously.

Afterwards, when three months later the dreadful news came that her father had been killed in a volcanic eruption on one of the mountains he was exploring, she thought she must have had a presentiment that he would never return from that particular expedition.

When he said goodbye to her, she had clung to him frantically, feeling in some strange way that he was slipping away from her, not only physically, but as if there was never any future for them together.

"Do not forget your promise that we will go exploring the moment I finish here!" she had said over and over again.

Yet even as she said it something deep within her heart told her that, whatever her father's reply, it was something that would never happen.

It was impossible to think of him as dead because he had always been so vital and magnetic in a way that was difficult to explain to other people who had no magnetism and who, to Ilita, often seemed little more than morons with whom it was impossible to communicate.

Then as her first misery lightened a little and she forced herself to concentrate on her work, she knew that, just as she had known after her mother's death, her father was still near her, and that still, in some strange way she could not describe in words, she could communicate with him.

At night she would lie thinking of him until she could see his face etched in the darkness in front of her, and he would be smiling at her in his irresistible way, which always seemed part of the sunshine as he said:

"Look forward – not back!"

"That is what I have to do," Ilita told herself, but what she had to look for or what she had expected to find, was a question to which there was no answer.

She received a letter from her father's younger brother who had now succeeded and was the Sixth Earl of Darrington.

It was a somewhat cold letter telling her that he deeply regreted his brother's death, but he was glad to think she was well looked after in such an exceptional school, and if there was anything she wanted she could get in touch with him.

There was no mention, Ilita noticed, of his being anxious to see her, and she wondered whether he intended, when her schooldays were finished, that she should live with him and her Aunt Sybil.

It was something, she was sure, they would dislike and so would she, but she cheered herself up with the thought that her godmother had promised to look after her in London as soon as she was of age to be a débutante, and as Mrs. Van Holden had no children, she would perhaps, when she returned to America, take her with her.

'That would be rather exciting,' Ilita thought and she sat down and wrote to Mrs. Van Holden telling her what had happened.

It took a long time for her letter to cross the Atlantic and for her to receive a reply, but the letter she eventually received from her godmother said everything she had hoped.

Mrs. Van Holden was naturally horrified at the news of her father's death and, although she did not say so in her letter, Ilita had the idea that she was actually delighted that now she had the title and was, of course, socially far more important than she had been before as merely the daughter of a younger son of a peer.

She had, since she arrived at the Convent, written to her godmother every month to tell her how she was getting on and the work she was doing.

She felt it was something she must do since her godmother was paying for her education, and the least she would expect was a regular report on her progress.

Mrs. Van Holden had answered every letter Ilita had written to her until six months ago. Then there had been a long silence and she had written anxiously asking if she had received her letters, or perhaps she had been travelling and they had not been redirected.

She finally had a letter from a secretary who told her that her godmother had been recently widowed and was deeply distressed at losing her husband and was not in good health herself.

She, however, sent her love and begged Ilita to write again as soon as possible.

Ilita did so, increasing her letters to one a week but finding it hard to think of interesting things to tell someone on the other side of the world.

Over the following two or three months she had received two short letters written by Mrs. Van Holden in a very shaky hand.

"I am getting better, dear child," she had said, "and of course, I am hurrying to be well enough to come to England to meet you in London when you leave the Convent. I have already told them to find me a large house that I can rent for the Season where I can give the Ball I promised for you. I have also written to your

22

Uncle's wife, the new Countess, to ask if she intends to present you at Buckingham Palace."

It all sounded very exciting, but then a month ago Ilita had received a letter from her aunt.

It had obviously been dictated to a secretary and was brisk, cold and business-like. It informed Ilita that she had just learnt that her godmother, Mrs. Van Holden, had just died in Virginia and was therefore not coming to London as had been planned.

"It had been arranged," the letter went on, "that you should stay in London with Mrs. Van Holden. However, I have also had a communication from the Mother Superiour at your school in which she informs me that you are now too old to remain there as a pupil and they will therefore be sending you back to England at the end of the term. You will come here to me at Darrington House and I will then inform you of what has been decided about your future. I do not wish you, until I have seen you, to communicate with any other members of the family. When I know what time the train on which you will be travelling reaches Victoria, I will send a carriage to meet you. Kindly follow the instructions in this letter.

Yours sincerely,

Sybil Darrington."

Ilita read the letter over and over again, thinking it extraordinary that her aunt should write to her so formally.

She remembered that when she heard of the death of her uncle two months earlier and had written a conventional letter of condolence, she had had no reply.

This did not particularly surprise her because she had not had any communication from her father's family, except the one formal letter after his death.

She knew her godmother had written to her aunt and uncle telling them what she was planning on her behalf, but she did not know whether they were pleased or not at the idea of someone outside the family presenting her to Society.

She could remember that when she had last seen her

aunt she had thought her very beautiful, but at the same time she had a sharp, rather hard voice and her father had definitely disliked her.

"She is very lovely, Papa," Ilita had said.

"So is a cobra when you do not see its tongue!" her father answered and they had both laughed.

Now as she thought of meeting her aunt, Ilita felt herself shiver! Then the train came to a standstill and the Italian girl, jumping and shouting for joy, sprang on to the platform to fling her arms around her mother's neck.

Ilita and the Sister were alone in the compartment.

"Thank you, Sister, for looking after me," Ilita said in her soft voice. "It has been a very long journey for you, and I am afraid you will be tired if you are returning immediately."

"I will be all right," Sister Angelica replied. "But you must take care of yourself, my dear. Remember your prayers and that God is always looking after you."

"I hope so," Ilita said.

As if she knew what she was feeling, Sister Angelica suddenly and unexpectedly put her hand on her shoulder.

"You have worked hard, my child," she said. "We all have our crosses to bear, but the light is always there if we ask for it."

It was such an unexpected thing for Sister Angelica to say that for a moment Ilita looked at her in astonishment, and then she said with a little tremor in her voice:

"Thank you, Sister."

"You will always be in my prayers," Sister Angelica smiled, "so do not be afraid."

A porter found Ilita's trunks and when he had piled them on his trolley, she followed him outside the station.

Among the carriages waiting there she saw one with the Darrington crest painted on the door.

There was, as she expected, a thin, grey-haired man who introduced himself as a secretary.

"I did not come to the platform, My Lady, in case I should miss you," he said. "In fact your aunt instructed me to wait by the carriage.

"I am glad to find you here," Ilita said, "and I am afraid I have rather a lot of luggage."

Her trunks did not only contain clothes which she was certain would not be suitable for the fashionable world, but books and many souvenirs of Florence that she could not bear to leave behind.

Because her godmother had been so generous not only in paying her school fees, but also in providing her with quite a large amount of pocket-money every month, she had bought pictures as well as books and other things that were particularly Florentine.

It would have been impossible to resist the glorious coloured silks which were depicted in so many of the portraits by the great Masters, or the curiously carved little pieces of coral with which the shops on the Ponte Vecchio were filled.

"If you ask me," one of Ilita's friends had said, "you would be better off buying yourself a new bonnet!"

"These will last when the bonnet will be out of fashion," Ilita had laughed.

She knew the truth was that as she had no home, the little things she acquired were the only possessions that were her own and which she cherished because they had memories that no one could take away from her.

The same applied to some of the things she possessed of her mother's, which were not valuable, except in sentiment and affection.

Her trunks were piled on the back of the carriage and even then several boxes had to come inside to be placed on the small seat opposite where she was sitting with her aunt's secretary beside her.

"Will you tell me your name?" Ilita asked politely.

"Shepherd," he replied. "I have been in charge of Darrington House for many years. In fact, I ran it when your Ladyship's grandfather was alive, and hoped to continue with your father had he not met such an untimely death."

"I am sure Papa would have been very glad to have you to help him," Ilita said. "He would have found it very strange to be the owner of two large houses after never being quite certain where we would be sleeping the next night!"

Mr. Shepherd smiled.

"Actually, My Lady, the Earl of Darrington owns twenty houses in different parts of the country."

Ilita gave a little gasp.

"That is too many!"

"Something I have often thought myself," Mr. Shepherd agreed, "and of course, now I have to keep them in working order for his present Lordship who is only thirteen."

"I do not think I have ever met my cousin," Ilita said.

"He is a very charming young man," Mr. Shepherd said, "but I regret to say that he has not benefited by his education, as you have, My Lady. If you do not think it impertinent, I was extremely impressed by the achievements the Mother Superior listed in her last letter to Her Ladyship."

Ilita longed to ask if her aunt had been impressed too, but as Mr. Shepherd did not volunteer the information, she was too shy to enquire.

It did not take long for the two well-bred horses to carry them from the station up the hill to Hyde Park Corner and into Park Lane.

Ilita wanted to look out of the window and remember the places she had seen before – the green of the park, the houses looking over it, all of which belonged, she knew, to the most important members of the aristocracy.

Instead she only knew that she was nervous and extremely afraid of what lay ahead.

It was almost as if she had a presentiment that it was not going to be pleasant meeting her aunt, nor would her plans for her future be in any way to her liking.

Then she told herself she was being ridiculous.

If her aunt did not want her, and that was perhaps understandable, there must be quite a number of the family who would welcome her for her father's sake, even though he had outlawed himself for so many years from his cousins, aunts, and uncles and what he often referred to as a "a whole clan of Darrington-Coombes".

"They are puffing up with pride," he had said once, "and think their blue blood entitles them to look down their noses at everyone else. I can tell you, my dearest, that I get far more enjoyment in the company of an Arab Sheik or an Indian Fakir, than I do listening to my kith and kin droning on about their own importance. I know when you meet them you will feel the same."

It was all very well, Ilita thought now, for her father to have felt so independent, and she could understand in a way how, like a naughty little boy playing truant, it had amused him to run away from everything that had been so important to his father and all the generations before him.

But he was a man, and suddenly she felt that London was very large and she was very small. It was all so frightening and unfamiliar, and she felt more alone than she had ever been in her life.

"Help me, Papa! Please help me!" she cried desperately in her heart as the horses came to a standstill outside a large, porticoed front door.

"Here we are, My Lady," Mr. Shepherd said in what she thought was a deliberately encouraging tone, as he stepped out first to help her alight.

"Thank you for meeting me," Ilita said a little breathlessly.

"It has been a pleasure," Mr. Shepherd replied, "and I think you will find Her Ladyship waiting for you upstairs."

Slowly Ilita walked into the house, across the marble hall where four footmen, wearing what she knew was the Darrington uniform with its crested buttons and striped blue and yellow waistcoats, were waiting.

A man in a frock coat, looking rather like a Bishop, came towards her slowly.

"Good afternoon, M'Lady, and welcome back to England! I hope Your Ladyship's journey was not too arduous."

"This is Bateson," Mr. Shepherd said at Ilita's elbow. "He has been at Darrington House for many years, and of course remembers your father."

"I do indeed, M'Lady," Bateson said. "We were all deeply distressed to hear of his death."

"Thank you," Ilita said.

Bateson walked a little ahead of her and she understood she was to follow him upstairs.

He moved slowly as if he found the stairs hard for his legs which she suspected were getting old.

He did not say any more, and when they reached the first landing he walked along a corridor she vaguely remembered led to the Master Bedroom in the house which overlooked the garden at the back.

The last time she had been there she had been very small and had come with her father to say goodbye to her grandfather and grandmother before they left London on one of his journeys to the East.

She remembered that her grandfather had been extremely angry, declaring her father was wasting his time gadding about the world instead of settling down and taking an interest in politics.

"They bore me stiff," she could hear her father saying defiantly and aggressively, but at the same time with a little twinkle in his eyes.

"It is the duty of everyone in our position to help run this country!" the Earl of Darrington had said ponderously.

Ilita could not remember what her father's reply had been, but of course nothing could alter his decision to visit Ceylon and they had set off the next morning, to travel uncomfortably in second-rate ships because they could not afford better ones, yet enjoying every moment of the voyage and the land they discovered when the journey ended.

The Butler was opening a high mahogany door, and as Ilita moved forward she heard him announce in stentorian tones:

"Lady Ilita Darrington-Coombe, M'Lady, has just arrived."

28

Chapter Two

For a moment everything seemed to swim in front of Ilita's eyes.

Then she managed to see, through the rays of the sun coming through the window, that her aunt was seated elegantly on a *chaise longue* at the far end of the room.

She walked towards her aware as she did so that the Countess was looking at her critically until she reached her side.

Then as the door shut behind her and they were alone Ilita said:

"Good afternoon, Aunt Sybil, and thank you for sending a carriage to meet me."

For a moment there was silence. Then as her aunt looked her over in a way that Ilita felt was distinctly hostile, she said sharply:

"Sit down, I have something to say to you."

Ilita obeyed, sitting on the edge of an armchair that was nearest to the *chaise longue*.

As she did so she realised how beautiful her aunt was, and how expensively and fashionably dressed.

For the first time since she had left the Convent she was aware that her travelling-gown of pale blue material with a cloak over it was very schoolgirlish and not at all what she might be expected to wear in London.

She had told herself before she left that it would be absurb to spend the little money she had left in buying clothes in Florence when she was quite certain that what she required in London would be very different.

But she had not really thought about it very seriously, somehow supposing that the right gowns would be provided for her in the same way that her godmother, Mrs. Van Holden, had provided everything she required when she had arrived at the Convent.

Now she felt uncomfortably that perhaps she might at least have made an effort to buy something smarter, and a better trimmed bonnet.

She thought perhaps her aunt was criticising her for looking somewhat shabby and not in keeping with the grandeur of the house.

Then the Countess began to speak in a sharp, hard voice:

"I do not know, Ilita," she said, "whether you have considered what you will do in the future now that your godmother is dead, and there is no question of your entering Society as she had planned."

Ilita did not know what to answer to this and was therefore silent as her aunt went on:

"I had expected of course, that Mrs. Van Holden, who was a rich woman, would pay for everything including your gowns and for the Ball which she intended to give for you, and you were to stay with her while she was in London."

"I am very sad that she is dead," Ilita said, "for as you know, Aunt Sybil, she was very kind to me."

"Very kind indeed!" the Countess agreed aggressively, as if Ilita was arguing about it. "However, at least now you are on your own you should be able to put the education she paid for to some use."

"I was wondering," Ilita said hesitatingly, "where you would . . want me to . . live."

"I can answer that question quite easily," her aunt replied, "and that is – not here! I have no intention, Ilita, of saddling myself with any impecunious member of the Darrington-Coombe family, or of being responsible at my age for someone who requires to be chaperoned."

There was a note in her voice which told Ilita only too well how much she disliked the idea.

She was now more certain than she had been before her arrival that her aunt disliked her personally.

"Perhaps, Aunt Sybil," she ventured slowly, "there is

some member of . . Papa's family who would . . like me to live . . with them."

"If there is I have no idea who it might be," the Countess said. "You can hardly expect anyone to want a penniless relation thrust upon them, especially as your father went out of his way to ignore or antagonise all his relatives for so many years."

"Then if there is . . nobody with whom I can . . live," Ilita said in a frightened tone, "where am I to go?"

"That is just what I am going to tell you," the Countess said, "and I have, I may say, given the matter a great deal of thought."

She paused as if she was choosing her words carefully before she said:

"There would be a great deal of unpleasant gossip, and it might even get into the newspapers, if you were drifting about the place not being properly chaperoned and, I dare say, getting into trouble of one sort or another."

Ilita drew in her breath as if she would protest, but her Aunt continued before she could speak:

"It was certainly something your father always managed to do, and there has been quite enough gossip about him in the past without your adding to it."

"I was not thinking of . . doing so," Ilita said humbly, "and can you tell me please, Aunt Sybil . . if Papa has left me any money?"

"Left you any money?" the Countess enquired. "Of course not! You must be aware that he lived on an allowance which he received through the generosity of his father, even though he violently disapproved of the way his son wandered about the world instead of settling down at home as he should have done."

"Papa was very happy in his explorations," Ilita said, feeling she must stick up for her father.

"I am sure he was," the Countess said sarcastically, "but that does not mean that you are anything but an encumbrance without a penny to bless yourself with!"

The way she spoke made Ilita grip her fingers together and force herself not to reply, knowing it would do no

31

good and only make her aunt more aggresive than she was already.

"I am sure," she managed to say humbly, "that Papa did not . . mean to die and leave me . . unprovided for."

"Nevertheless that is what he has done!" the Countess said. "As far as I can ascertain he has nothing in the Bank, and when I last spoke with the family Solicitors they were still looking for his will which apparently he omitted to make."

There was no answer to this and after a moment Ilita said:

"What do you . . want me to do, Aunt Sybil?"

"As I have already said, I have given it a great deal of thought," the Countess answered, "and at first I thought the best thing for you would be, as you have been apparently so happy in a Convent, to become a Nun."

For a moment Ilita was speechless, then with a little cry that seemed to echo round the room she exclaimed:

"But . . Aunt Sybil . . I could not do that! I have no wish to be a Nun and no . . calling for it."

"It is not a question of what you wish or do not wish!" the Countess said sharply. "Before we go any further, I would point out, Ilita, that as your father is dead and so is your Uncle, I am now your guardian until my son Anthony comes of age, which will not be for a very long time. You, therefore, have to do what I tell you and obey me. That is the law!"

"B.but . . I cannot be a Nun!" Ilita cried.

"I understand there are difficulties, especially as you are not a Catholic," the Countess conceded, "and I have therefore decided that you must earn your living one way or another, I must find you some work at which I must suppose you would prove to be efficient."

Ilita drew in her breath and gripped her fingers until the nails dug into the softness of her flesh.

It was not so much what she was saying, but the contemptuous way in which she was speaking that told her the Countess was sentencing her to a life which was bound to be unpleasant, and against which she had no appeal.

Finally, as her aunt did not speak, she said:

"Will you tell me, Aunt Sybil, what you have . . planned for me to do?"

"It was certainly not easy to think of any place in England where you would not be a nuisance and where I should not be continually anxious in case your identity was discovered."

"M.my . . identity?"

"You do not suppose, you stupid child, that I want people saying that my husband's niece, Lady Ilita Darrington-Coombe, has to earn her own living, and suggesting that I should make myself responsible for you?"

"Then . . what do you . . propose?" Ilita asked.

"It was just by chance," the Countess replied, "that I discovered that a friend of mine, the Marchioness of Lyss, nine months ago was stricken with blindness. She was a great beauty, and appalled by what has happened she has gone into seclusion where she sees no one and has no wish for anybody's sympathy."

As she spoke the Countess did not sound at all sympathetic, but rather as if she thought it was extremely careless or foolish of her friend to have got into such a position.

"I therefore wrote to the Marchioness," the Countess went on, "suggesting that in view of her condition she might find it helpful to employ a reader, and in that way keep in touch with world events."

"A . . a reader!" Ilita whispered beneath her breath.

"I told her," the Countess went on, "and of course you must not deny this, that I have employed you myself in one way or another, and found you very satisfactory. In fact, I shall give you an excellent reference!"

"I . . I do not . . understand," Ilita said helplessly. "Am I to live with this lady . . and just read to her? It is something I have . . never heard of before."

"How could you, when you have been living in uncivilised parts of the world where I doubt whether the type of people with whom your father associated had servants of any sort, let alone the more cultured ones?"

33

Ilita could not answer this because she thought it would be undignified. Instead she said:

"And you think your friend will just want me to read to her from the newspapers and books?"

"I expect, if she has any sense, she will find dozens of other things to occupy you," the Countess said sharply. "After all, like everybody else in the world, she will expect value for money, and I did say in my reference that you were a good sewer."

The Countess's voice sharpened as she went on:

"I have always been told that is something they teach well at the Convent, and will certainly be more useful to you in the future than all those high-sounding prizes you have won for the subjects which, as far as I can ascertain, are not likely to be worth a penny-piece in the market-place!"

"I had hoped that my godmother would be pleased that I had done well in my lessons at the Convent," Ilita said.

"Well, she is dead, and we cannot know if she is pleased or not!" the Countess retorted. "What we do know is that you have to earn your own living, and you will have no help from me, except that I am prepared to write you references which will ensure your employment."

"I . . I never thought of . . anything like this!" Ilita said more to herself than to her aunt.

"Well, the sooner you begin to think about it the better!" her aunt said. "As I have said, from now on you will be on your own, you you will have to learn to make the best of your opportunities, and be grateful for them, whatever they may be."

As she spoke the Countess looked at Ilita sitting opposite her and her eyes hardened.

With the sunshine on her face she looked very young and lovely.

Her eyes that in some lights were grey and in others purple, were young and frightened, and the dark lashes curling up in a child-like way were tipped with gold to match the gold of her hair showing beneath her plain bonnet.

She looked fragile and somehow insubstantial, and yet she had a youthful beauty which the Countess recognised was something she had lost many years earlier.

Because the thought infuriated her she said:

"At least the Marchioness will not be able to see you and be irritated, as I am, by that ridiculous baby face of yours! You have to grow up and cope with the world, and the sooner you realise that the better!"

"You said, Aunt Sybil, that I was not to . . use my own . . name," Ilita faltered.

"Get this into your head once and for all, that from the moment you leave this house you are no longer a Darrington-Coombe, and I forbid you – do you hear me? – I forbid you to try to get in touch with any of your father's relatives! Not that I think they would be interested in you if you did."

"Who . . am I to . . be?"

"I have already chosen a name for you, something quiet and unassuming. In fact, it is the name of a Lady's-maid I once had. When I wrote to the Marchioness I told her that the woman I am recommending is called 'Marsh'."

"Marsh?" Ilita asked. "But . . why Marsh?"

"It is as good a name as any!" the Countess snapped. "Make quite certain, Ilita, you do not forget that it is your name and that you come from one of the villages on the Darrington-Coombe estate. You belong to a middle-class family, but your parents are dead. There is no need for anybody to know anything else about you."

Ilita felt as if her head was swimming, and she could not believe what she was hearing.

It had been bad enough to think as she travelled across Europe in the train that she was an orphan in what she sensed would be a hostile world.

But at least she could be herself; at least she could belong to the two people who had loved her, her father and mother, and could hold up her head proudly because her blood was their blood.

Now she was forbidden to think of them and must be instead some person of unknown origin called Marsh who existed only in the Countess's imagination.

She felt every nerve in her body tense to the point where she wanted to spring up and say she would not do it. She would defy her aunt and somehow, although she was not certain how, she would find some of her father's relations and throw herself upon their mercy.

As if what she was thinking communicated itself to her aunt without words, the Countess said:

"If you do not obey me, then you may be certain that I will put my other suggestion into operation. I will find a Convent that will take you, and in which you will be enclosed for the rest of your life! I have a feeling it will not be difficult to do, if I make a contribution to the Convent funds."

She spoke reflectively as if she was thinking it out, and Ilita, frightened, said quickly:

"No . . no! I will do what you tell me to do, Aunt Sybil, and go as a reader to this lady who is blind."

"Make no mistake," her Aunt warned, "if you are sent away for incompetence or because you do not please the Marchioness of Lyss, I shall make quite certain that such a situation does not arise for a second time. Do you understand?"

"I . . I understand."

"Very well!"

Her aunt glanced at the clock.

"You will now go to the room which has been prepared for you here in the house," she said. "As you are obviously tired after your long journey, you will stay there and your evening meal will be brought to you. Tomorrow morning you will be conveyed to the station where you will take a train to the halt at Lyss Castle, which is in Oxfordshire. I have already informed the Marchioness's secretary what time you will be arriving, and doubtless there will be some kind of conveyance to meet you."

Ilita felt that this was the end of the conversation with her aunt and she said quickly:

"There is . . one thing I must ask you . . Aunt Sybil."

"What is that?"

"Could you let me have some . . money . . just a little? I am afraid I have come from Florence with practically nothing, as I had some presents to buy before I left."

"I am surprised you could afford to be so extravagant," her aunt said sarcastically. "You will of course be paid a salary in your position as reader, but I have decided, out of the kindness of my heart, for which I hope you will be sincerely grateful, to allow you £50 a year so long as you keep your promise to be anonymous and not let anyone in any circumstances be aware of your true identity."

Her voice rose as she went on:

"Should I hear so much as a whisper that you have been indiscreetly confidential, make no mistake, I shall stop the £50 and begin my search for a suitable Convent."

"I . . I promise you I will . . be very discreet," Ilita said.

Her aunt reached out beside her to where on a small table there was a sealed envelope.

"I have put £25 in this envelope for you," she said, "and you will receive another £25 in cash – there is no question of your having a cheque – in six months' time. But make sure, Ilita, that in the meantime you keep the position I have found for you. I have no wish for you to come running back asking me for further references or for more money, which you will *not* receive!"

"I will . . try not to do that, Aunt Sybil."

Her aunt watched her as she rose to take the envelope from her hand. Then she said:

"I will not see you again, there is no point in my doing so. I have done what is best in the circumstances, and you should be grateful. After all, in the position in which you find yourself, you have no one to blame but your selfish, inconsiderate father!"

Ilita drew in her breath.

She hated to hear her father spoken of in such a way, but she knew there was no point in arguing.

She merely took the envelope which she would have liked to refuse, but she knew it would be a stupid thing to do, and then walked towards the door.

As she reached it she looked back.

"Goodbye, Aunt Sybil," she said.

"Just remember what I have told you," the Countess said sharply.

Ilita let herself out and found as she had half-expected there was a housemaid waiting in the corridor outside who dropped her a curtsy.

"I've been told to take you to the House-keeper, M'Lady," she said, "who has had a room prepared for Your Ladyship."

"Thank you," Ilita answered.

She walked along the corridor and up a staircase to the second floor where she knew the less important bedrooms would be situated.

Waiting at the top of the stairs was an elderly woman with white hair, wearing a rustling black silk gown with the silver chatelaine at her waist.

Ilita looked at her, then gave a little cry of delight.

"Mrs. Fielding! It *is* Mrs. Fielding, is it not?"

"It is indeed, M'Lady!" Mrs. Fielding replied. "Fancy your remembering me after so many years!"

"I remember how kind you were when I last came here," Ilita said. "You gave me a box of gingerbread to take away with me."

"So I did!" Mrs. Fielding said. "Now come along, M'Lady. I've a room ready for you, and Your Ladyship will certainly want a rest after such a long journey."

She took Ilita into a prettily decorated bedroom which also looked out over the garden.

She noticed that only one of her trunks had been brought upstairs and guessed as the household knew she would be leaving first thing in the morning that somebody had been sensible enough to unpack only what was absolutely necessary.

"Well, you've grown into a lovely young lady, and no mistake!" Mrs. Fielding was saying. "I always thought you'd resemble your mother, God rest her soul, but there's a bit of your father there too, and there never was a more handsome boy than he was when I first sees him."

"You must tell me about Papa when he was a boy," Ilita

said softly. "There is nobody to talk to me about him now."

"I know, M'Lady, and it's hard, real hard!" Mrs. Fielding said. "We were all hoping you'd be staying here, but Her Ladyship says you're going to friends in the country, not wishing to be in London without your father and mother to look after you."

"Yes . . that is right," Ilita agreed.

She had wondered what explanation her aunt would have made to the servants.

"Well, your father was never one for the city," Mrs. Fielding chattered on. "He wanted to be riding, swimming or climbing trees. Never still for a minute, he was, and that full of mischief you never knew what he was up to next!"

Ilita pulled off her bonnet and sat down on the bed to listen.

For the first time since she had come into the house the fear that had gripped her all the time she was with her aunt seemed to recede a little, and she felt a slight warmth return as she listened to Mrs. Fielding chattering on.

"I could hardly believe it was true when they told me your father was dead, when we were all so pleased that he was to be the new Earl!"

"I think Papa would have found the position rather restricting," Ilita said.

Mrs. Fielding laughed.

"Maybe he would. At the same time, he always had a kind word and a smile for everybody, which is different from other people I could mention!"

Mrs. Fielding pressed her lips together as if she felt she had said too much and Ilita said:

"Thank you for bringing my trunk upstairs. It was clever of you to realise that was the trunk I would want for tonight."

"I had to admit we had to look in two or three before we found the right one," Mrs. Fielding said. "You might be setting up home, M'Lady, with all those books and other things you've got with you!"

"They are the only home I have now," Ilita said sadly.

Mrs. Fielding picked up the cape which Ilita had taken from her shoulders.

She must have realised as she did so that it had seen better days.

"What would you wish to wear tomorrow, M'Lady, to go to the country?" she asked.

"I shall have to wear what I am wearing today," Ilita said. "I am afraid that most of my clothes, Mrs. Fielding, are somewhat out of date, but I thought it would be an extravagance to buy new things in Florence when I was coming to London."

She thought she must add some other explanation and she said quickly:

"But my aunt says there is no time for shopping, so I must just make do with what I have."

She looked down at the trunk that had been opened by Mrs. Fielding, and Ilita was certain she thought that her school-girl clothes, some of which had grown a little tight for her and which were very plain and simple, were in fact too young for her.

There was a little pause. Then Mrs. Fielding said:

"It doesn't seem right, M'Lady, that you should go away empty-handed, as you might say, and I'm sure your friends in the country will expect you to look fashionable and up-to-date."

"Well they will be disappointed," Ilita said wryly, "but I expect, as I am skilful with my needle, that I will be able to alter my gowns, let them out and add a little decoration to them."

She thought as she spoke that she would certainly not do anything extravagant.

If she had only £25 to last her for the next six months she would have to plan every penny she spent very carefully. Anyway, nobody would expect a reader, who was only a superior servant, to be fashionably dressed.

Mrs. Fielding was standing over the trunk with a worried expression on her face.

"You say you're good at sewing, M'Lady?"

"Very good, as it happens," Ilita answered. "I won first prize at the Convent for my embroidery and for my plain stitching, and also I am quite proficient at making gowns."

She laughed as she explained:

"That sounds strange in a Convent but every year at Christmas we produced one of Shakespeare's Plays. We not only painted the scenery, but also made the gowns. As I made them better than most of the girls, I was appointed wardrobe mistress."

"Well, I never!" Mrs. Fielding said. "That makes it easy for me to help you, M'Lady."

"How can you do that?" Ilita asked.

Mrs. Fielding looked towards the door to see that it was shut. Then she said:

"I've got some rolls of rather pretty muslins which Her Ladyship has bought over the years for curtains, either for the windows or for beds. I'm sure if we ask her she would say she had forgotten they ever existed. What I suggest is we cut off some yards from the muslins you like best, and you can make yourself gowns, if it's not easy for you living in the country to get to the shops."

Ilita felt certain Mrs. Fielding was being tactful, for the servants who knew everything, would be aware that her father had left her no money, and her aunt was determined to do as little for her as possible.

Her father had often said:

"People talk about spies and espionage, but what they forget is that in every household there is a whole army of spies who see everything, hear everything, and from whom no secret can ever be hidden."

"I presume you are talking about the staff," her mother said.

"Of course I am," her father replied, "and you, my darling, know as well as I do that the servants in your house and in mine knew of our marriage long before it was officially announced in the newspapers."

Her mother had laughed.

"That is certainly true, and they found it very romantic, which is more than my father did."

They both laughed. Then her father put his arms around her mother to say:

"And you also found it romantic, my precious?"

"I found it the most wonderful thing that could happen to any woman," her mother replied with a little throb in her voice.

Because she had not forgotten those happy days, Ilita said quickly:

"If you could really bring me some muslin, Mrs. Fielding, I would be very grateful, but I would not wish to upset Aunt Sybil."

"She will not know, M'Lady, you can be certain of that! Now you wait here, and I'll bring you what I think you'll find most useful."

*   *   *

It was certainly a consolation to Ilita before she went to sleep that night to feel that thanks to Mrs. Fielding she would not need many new gowns in her position as reader.

The Housekeeper had come back into her bedroom carrying several rolls of material in her arms while a young housemaid behind her had another half-a-dozen.

There was muslin embroidered with little flowers all over it, which had been intended to decorate the crib in the Nursery before Anthony was born, but had then been discarded as being too feminine.

There was a pretty white muslin with frills that was meant to be draped from a corola over a bed.

Other muslins were for inside curtains to soften the impact of the heavy damask ones which blocked out the light.

Mrs. Fielding and Ilita chose enough for five gowns which would, she thought, look very becoming, especially when the Housekeeper also found a few rolls of satin ribbon which could be added to them.

"How can I thank you for being so kind?" she asked, when the muslins which were not required had been taken away.

"I'd like to see you, M'Lady, looking as lovely as your mother looked when your father brought her here to see your grandfather, the old Earl. Very angry he was, when he heard they wished to be married!"

" 'What are you going to live on? That's what I'd like to know?' he asked, and we could hear his voice shouting the words from the study door which was open."

"I am sure Papa and Mama did not worry about that," Ilita said.

"That's the truth, M'Lady! Whatever His Lordship said it made no impression on them, and they came out of the Study hand-in-hand, looking so happy it brought the tears to my eyes."

" 'Wish us happiness, Fieldy,' your father said, which was what he always called me.

" 'You know I wish you that, Mr. Marcus,' I replied. 'And where will you be living?'

" 'In a Heaven of our own,' your father says, 'whether it be on the top of a mountain, or at the bottom of the ocean, but we will be together, Fieldy, and very, very happy!' "

Mrs. Fielding put her hand up to her eyes to wipe away a tear before she said:

"Then they looked into each other's eyes and forgot I was there. I knew your father was right, and they'd be living in a Heaven of their own."

"And that is exactly what they did," Ilita said, "and I was with them."

She jumped off the bed as she spoke and walked to the window so that Mrs. Fielding would not see her unhappiness.

Looking back it had been Heaven, but now it was 'Paradise Lost', and something she would never find again.

"How could you have died and left me alone, Papa?" she asked in her heart as she had asked so often.

Then once again she could see his eyes twinkling at her and hear him say with laughter in his voice:

"Look forward. There is always something new beyond the horizon."

"And what will that be?" Ilita asked herself.

She knew that when she left Darrington House tomorrow the future for her would be even more frightening than it had seemed before she arrived.

* * *

It was a feeling which seemed to grow during the night as she lay finding it hard to sleep, and when morning came and there were only Mrs. Fielding and Mr. Shepherd to say goodbye to her, she felt as if she was setting out on an expedition.

But she had no map, no compass, and certainly no guide to accompany her.

She knew her new life had started when Mr. Shepherd put her into the train at Paddington and waved her goodbye as she was carried away from him out of the station.

It was inconceivable that anyone of her age should be expected to travel alone without even a maid to accompany her.

But in her new position as a servant, whatever high-sounding title might be attached to it, she was expected to look after herself and not require a chaperon, to which she was really entitled as a Lady of Quality.

"I must remember my name is Marsh," Ilita told herself.

Now that she was really on her own, she could not help recalling over and over again the threat in her aunt's voice as she had said:

"One hint that you have been indiscreet and you will be incarcerated in a Convent for the rest of your life!"

She was not so foolish as not to realise that her aunt's threats were very real.

A guardian had complete control over a girl of eighteen, and there would be no one to dispute whatever her aunt decided was best for her.

There would be no one to whom she could appeal if she was in fact taken to a Convent and enrolled as a postulant.

She was quite certain too that it would not be a Convent

at all like the one in which she had been living in Florence.

That was very different. To begin with it was very rich, heavily endowed by the city as well as by those who were grateful for the education it had given their daughters.

Ilita had never been allowed to enter the enclosed side of the Convent where the Nuns prayed incessantly and never left the Convent walls.

But she knew that many of them came from the richest and most aristocratic families in Italy.

The pupils whispered amongst themselves that many of the Nuns, whom they saw only in Chapel and at no other time, had taken the veil because they had been crossed in love, or had lost their husbands at a very early age.

To Ilita it had always seemed a waste of what her father had called "the joy of living".

He had exuded happiness to all with whom he came in contact because he was so alive, because he enjoyed everything so tremendously, and because he somehow inspired people through the happiness that seemed to envelop him and his family.

"Being with you, Marcus, is a better tonic than anything the doctors can give me," one of his friends told him once, and Ilita was sure it was meant literally and sincerely.

"The only trouble is," she had heard her father say, "that I shall not live long enough to do all the things I want to do."

"What sort of things are those, Papa?" she had asked him, knowing the answer.

"I have not yet been to China," he said, "and I must see the Great Wall before I die. I want to journey down the Nile, and I would like, too, to travel over Brazil. That is to mention just a few of the places I want to explore!"

Ilita slipped her hand into his.

"We will do it together, Papa."

"And that will be very exciting for both of us," her father promised.

"How can anything now be exciting without him?" she asked as the train puffed on through green fields and thick woodland.

But somehow she had to survive on her own outside the Convent in a land of which she was completely and utterly ignorant because it was England and so very different from the lands that she had explored with her father.

Quite suddenly she found herself wondering whether it would not be better to die so that she could be with her father and mother rather than alone without them.

Then even as the thought came to her she knew it was wicked and something her father would despise as cowardly if he knew of it.

She had to be brave, she had to go forward and not look back. She had to believe, as he believed, that there would always be something exciting round the next corner, over the horizon, and on the other side of the mountain.

"Help me, Papa. Oh, please, help me!" she whispered.

Then, because she could not prevent it and she was alone in the carriage, the tears ran down her cheeks.

Chapter Three

The Halt for Lyss Castle was quite impressive with flowers growing in large round tubs and what was obviously a luxurious waiting-room beside the ordinary offices.

There was one old porter on the station who looked surprised when Ilita stepped out of the train and told him she had some luggage in the van.

With difficulty he pulled the trunks on to the platform, then said to her enquiringly:

"Would ye be expectin' someun t' meet ye, Miss?"

"Yes, there should be a carriage from Lyss Castle."

The old porter shook his head.

"Bain't be one 'ere at t'moment."

Ilita looked helpless.

This was something she had not expected, and she had no idea what to do about it.

The old porter instantly became fatherly.

"Now don' ye worry, Miss. Oi 'spects one'll turn up in a minute or two."

"I hope so," Ilita replied.

She walked to the entrance to the Halt and looked out over the rolling countryside, its green fields and profusion of trees looking very lush after Italy.

Although there was a long white dusty road twisting away into the distance, there was no sign of any vehicle on it.

She walked back on to the platform to find the porter stacking her luggage tidily and said to him:

"If nobody comes for me, what shall I do?"

"Oi 'spects it's only a question o' waitin', Miss."

As if to confirm his own words he walked, as Ilita had done, to the entrance of the Halt.

Ilita, feeling there was no point in going there again so

soon, sat down on the wooden seat and wondered what she should do if nobody came to collect her.

It was then she heard the sound of wheels, and as she got to her feet the porter came back.

"There be neither sight nor sound o' anyone from th' Castle, Miss," he said, "but Farmer Giles says 'e'll take ye there, only 'e be in a hurry."

As he spoke, Farmer Giles, a heavily built, middle-aged man, appeared carrying a crate on to the platform, which Ilita guessed was to catch the next train.

He looked towards her, and said in what she thought was a grudging voice:

"As ye be stranded, Oi'll give ye a lift to the Castle. But we've to be quick about it, or Oi'll be late for th' milking."

"Thank you very much," Ilita said breathlessly.

She picked up one of her smaller pieces of luggage and carried it herself from the platform to where she saw waiting the farmer's high-sided cart drawn by two rough but sturdy horses.

It took the farmer and the porter a few minutes to pile all Ilita's luggage into the back. When they had finished, Ilita tipped the old man and said to him:

"Thank you very much for being so kind to me."

"It be a pleasure, Miss, an' ye tak' care o' yerself."

He touched his forelock as he spoke which made her feel he was apprehensive of what she would find at the Castle.

Then she thought she was being imaginative and climbed lightly up to sit on the high seat beside the farmer, who already had the reins in his hands.

They drove off, and because Ilita realised Farmer Giles was concentrating on getting the maximum amount of speed out of his horses, she kept silent.

She was, however, longing to ask questions about the countryside, the Castle, and everything which seemed so strange to her.

It was not until they passed through a small village of attractive black and white cottages with thatched roofs and turned in through huge gates surmounted by stone griffins that Farmer Giles said:

"'Ere we be, but Oi doubt if ye'll find th' Castle much to yer loiking."

"Why do you say that?" Ilita asked.

"Things ain't wat they used to be, not by a long chalk."

"In what way?"

The farmer did not answer and she thought he decided he had said too much already and preferred to remain silent.

She stared ahead apprehensively, until on her first glimpse of the house where her aunt had sent her to live, she thought it was too big, too frightening, and she would be lost in it completely.

It certainly was a large and very impressive piece of Georgian architecture with an entrance portico carried by six Corinthian pillars rising to a tremendous height over a flight of great stone steps.

The centre block of the house was flanked on either side by a large wing, each of them big enough, Ilita thought, to be a mansion in itself.

It was magnificent, and she supposed in its own way almost beautiful, but at the moment she would have given anything in the world for the small black Bedouin tent which she had shared in the desert with her father, and to know that he was with her and she was not alone.

Farmer Giles, having drawn his horses up with what was almost a flourish at the bottom of the steps, climbed down and started to carry Ilita's trunks half-way up them.

Ilita got out of the cart and he seemed surprised as she held out her hand.

"Thank you very much," she said. "It was so very kind of you to bring me here, when I know you are in a hurry. I am very grateful."

He shook her hand a little roughly, lifted his tweed hat a few inches off the front of his head, then clambered back into the cart and started off down the drive.

As she watched him disappearing amongst the trees, Ilita felt as if she had lost a friend, although he had certainly not been a very communicative one.

As she looked back at the house she realised the door was still closed, but she supposed there must be a bell or a knocker of some sort by which she could signify her arrival.

It suddenly struck her that perhaps her aunt had made a mistake and after all she was not expected, and that was why she had not been met at the Halt.

If that was so, what should she do?

Then she told herself she was just being foolish and she must make somebody inside the house realise she was there.

She started slowly to climb the steps and as she reached her luggage something made her look back down the drive. In the distance she could see horses coming between the trees just where she had seen those belonging to Farmer Giles disappear.

She wondered why he was returning. Perhaps she had left something behind in his cart, or he might even have brought her to the wrong house by mistake.

Then as the horses came nearer and she could see them more clearly, she realised they were a team of four.

The sunshine was glittering on their silver bridles and they were being driven by a Gentleman with his tall hat at an angle on his head.

Standing on the steps, Ilita watched the Chaise, which she realised it was, coming nearer and nearer until it drew up just below her.

Then a groom jumped down from the seat at the back and went to the horses' heads as the Gentleman who was driving them put down the reins and climbed to the ground.

It was then, as if he saw Ilita for the first time, that he stared at her in astonishment, and as he climbed the steps two at a time he said in what she thought was a hard, harsh voice:

"What are you doing here? And what is all that luggage?"

"I have . . come here," Ilita answered in a low voice,

"because I . . have been . . employed . . ."

"Employed?" the Gentleman interrupted. "Then if you are employed, what do you mean by coming to this door instead of the back entrance? Surely you know better than that?"

He spoke so sharply that Ilita could only stare at him with frightened eyes, aware that he was scowling, and because he seemed so tall and overpowering he appeared almost to menace her.

When she did not reply, he made a sound of exasperation before he said:

"I will see what all this is about!"

Moving quickly up the rest of the steps he opened the front door at the top of them.

As he did there must have been somebody opening it from inside at the same time, for Ilita heard the Gentleman say:

"What is going on? Why is there nobody at the door?"

Then before there could be an answer he added:

"Who are you? And where is Glover?"

"Mr. Glover's in th' Pantry, Sir."

"Then fetch him!" the Gentleman ordered. "And why are you not wearing a coat?"

There was no answer to this and Ilita, listening had the impression that whoever it was the Gentleman had spoken to, had run away.

But he could not have gone far before another voice said:

"I heard voices, what's happening?" Then in a different tone: "Why, it's you, M'Lord! We weren't expecting you!"

"That is obvious!" the Gentleman replied, who Ilita realised now must be the Marquis of Lyss.

Nobody had mentioned the Marquis to her, but she was quite certain from the way the Gentleman was behaving that he must be the owner of the house.

She thought apprehensively that it had not been a very auspicious way of meeting her host, if that was indeed who he was.

The Marquis was now speaking in a tone so loud it would have been impossible not to overhear him even if she had had no wish to eavesdrop.

"Why are there no footmen in the hall except that scallywag without a coat on? And what is a woman doing on the steps with a ton of luggage?"

The way he spoke made Ilita wish she could disappear into thin air, and she realised that through the open door an elderly man, who was obviously Glover, was peering at her.

"That must be th' lady we was told was coming, M'Lord, as a reader to Her Ladyship."

"Reader? What do you mean – reader? We have never needed one at the Castle before!"

There was a moment's pause, then Ilita heard Glover explain:

"Since Your Lordship's been abroad, you may not be aware that Her Ladyship's gone blind."

"Blind?"

There was no doubt of the astonishment in the Marquis's voice, and after a moment he asked:

"When did this happen, and how?"

"Her ladyship had a fall out riding, M'Lord, about nine months ago. Since then, she's been unable to see."

"I had no idea," the Marquis murmured, and now his voice was quieter.

Then he said:

"I should have thought Sheldon might have communicated the matter to me. However, I will see him and find out what is happening. Send him to me!"

There was silence for a moment. Then Glover said in a hesitating way:

"I don't think Mr. Sheldon has come downstairs yet, M'Lord."

"Not come downstairs? What is wrong with him?"

"He lays in late in th' morning, M'Lord."

"It is nearly noon!" The Marquis exclaimed. "Are you telling me that Sheldon had become so inattentive to his duties that he is not in his office at this hour of the morning?"

Again there was silence. Then Glover replied uncomfortably:

"I think you'll find, M'Lord, that since Your Lordship's been abroad, things have changed a great deal."

"They certainly have, if this is what I find on my return!" the Marquis said sharply.

Then as if he suddenly remembered Ilita was outside on the steps he said:

"I suppose Mrs. Lynton will be looking after this young woman and her pile of luggage? Send that half-dressed footman, if that is what he calls himself, to tell her I am here."

There was a long pause before the Butler said:

"Mrs. Lynton's in the Castle, M'Lord, but she's not working."

"Not working? Why not? You are not going to tell me that she, of all people, cannot get up in the morning!"

"No, no, M'Lord. It's not that. Her Ladyship dismissed her!"

"Dismissed Mrs. Lynton? I do not believe it!"

"What happened, M'Lord, was having lived in the Castle for nearly forty years, she had nowhere to go, and just retired to her own room."

"Send for her, Glover! Send for her at once!" the Marquis ordered. "I will deal with this!"

Ilita heard Glover give instructions to a footman, who was obviously somewhere near them, and then say to the Marquis:

"If only you'd let us know, M'Lord, we'd have had things in better shape for your arrival."

"I do not want things dressed up to impress me," the Marquis replied sharply. "I had expected to find that everything was as it had been before I went abroad and before my father's death."

He paused before he added:

"Now I look round, the place is dirty! Look at the dust on that chest! The windows need cleaning, and why are there ashes still in the fireplace?"

"Things have changed, M'Lord, and a number of the staff were told to leave."

"Who told them? Who gave the order?" the Marquis asked. Then he answered his own question by saying: "Her Ladyship! Of course! But the house is mine, Glover, and I cannot believe that you, of all people, could have allowed it to go to rack and ruin in this disgraceful manner!"

"I knew Your Lordship'd be upset about it, but there was nothing I could do. Things have been difficult, very difficult, and Mr. Sheldon's not in a fit state to cope with everything."

"By that I presume you mean that he drinks!" the Marquis said. "I rather suspected it before I went away, but not to this extent. What has been happening on the estate?"

"I'm afraid Your Lordshop may be a little upset . . ."

"A little!"

The Marquis's voice rose and then as if he forced himself to be more controlled he said:

"I realise it is my own fault for not having come home before. The first thing you can do, Glover, is to put your own department in order. How many footmen have you?"

"Three, M'Lord, but as there hasn't been much for them to do, I'm afraid they are not up to Your Lordship's standards."

"Then get ones who are, and see that they look better than that scarecrow, or he can take his marching orders!"

He must have been referring to the footman who Ilita supposed had gone upstairs to find Mrs. Lynton, for at that moment the Marquis's voice changed as he exclaimed:

"Lynty! Thank goodness you are still here! What has been happening? How could everything be in a mess like this just because I have been away?"

"That's the right word for it, M'Lord," a quiet voice

54

replied. "But now you're back, perhaps things will get back to what they were."

"You may be sure of that," the Marquis said, "and you and I will see to it together. In the meantime, there is a young woman sitting on the steps with a pile of luggage who Glover tells me is a reader."

"I did hear about it, M'Lord, but of course as I was 'retired' so to speak, I don't know what arrangements have been made for her."

"There is no question of your retiring, Lynty," the Marquis said. "Take over the household and run it as you always have, and I shall expect it to be back to normal by tomorrow or at least the day after."

Mrs. Lynton laughed.

"Now I know Your Lordship's home! You are just like your father. His Lordship always wanted everything done yesterday!"

"Then you know what I expect," the Marquis said, "and I hope the rooms in the house which I shall be using are cleaner than this!"

"I doubt it," Mrs. Lynton said, "but I'll send to the village, M'Lord, for those who were dismissed without notice, and without even a pension after they'd served the family faithfully for so many years!"

"That is something I shall see to immediately," the Marquis promised.

As he was speaking, two young men who Ilita thought must be footmen came through the door and down the steps.

As they picked up the first of her trunks she went ahead of them, seeing as she walked through the door an elderly woman who she knew was Mrs. Lynton.

She was dressed very much the same as Mrs. Fielding had been at Darrington House, except that there was no chatelaine at her waist, and she guessed it had been discarded because she was no longer employed.

As they faced each other Mrs. Lynton said:

"I think you must be Miss Marsh, and I must apologise, Miss, that you weren't met as you should have been at the Halt."

"A kind farmer gave me a lift," Ilita explained, "but I am afraid, as he was in a hurry, that he just left my luggage on the steps."

"Well, at least he brought you to the right place," Mrs. Lynton said consolingly, "and if you will follow me, Miss, I will show you to your rooms."

She walked up the staircase and Ilita walked behind her.

As she put her hand on the banister she turned to look back to where the Marquis was standing deep in conversation with the Butler.

She saw, as she had not been able to do when he accosted her in such a frightening manner, that he was in fact a handsome man, dressed in the height of fashion.

She thought there was something dynamic about him which might be intimidating but would certainly ensure that he got things his own way.

She was not surprised that he had protested about the dust in the hall which was lying quite thick on the chests and tables, and saw it had already soiled the gloved hand she had placed on the banisters.

She quickly followed Mrs. Lynton without holding on to the rail for support, and knew as she did so that she felt even more apprehensive about what lay ahead of her than she had before.

It was certainly not the reception she had expected at any house owned by a friend of her aunt.

She longed to ask why the Marquis had been away for so long, and why things had deteriorated so badly, but was too shy to question the Housekeeper.

The First Floor was very impressive with a high ceiling, and the corridor along which they were walking was decorated with magnificent pictures underneath which there stood some French furniture that was obviously very valuable.

But everything looked dusty, and she thought to herself that it would need an army of housemaids to get it clean and polished in the time the Marquis had demanded.

"I expect," Mrs. Lynton was saying in her quiet voice,

"that as Her Ladyship might wish you to read to her late at night, and perhaps during the night seeing that she doesn't sleep well, it would be wise for you to have a bedroom near to hers. I will therefore arrange for this room to be got ready for you as quickly as possible."

She opened a door as she spoke and Ilita saw it was not a very large room on the side of the corridor which she guessed faced the State Rooms.

The shutters were closed and the curtains drawn, but when Mrs. Lynton had pulled them back she could see there was a large, comfortable-looking brass bedstead with a frilled valance and curtains of a pretty patterned chintz, while the furniture was all she might have expected to find in any opulent household.

"There is also a Sitting-Room communicating with this room," Mrs. Lynton was saying, "and I expect, Miss Marsh, you would like to have somewhere where you could be on your own."

She spoke firmly, then in a different tone, looking at Ilita searchingly she said:

"Surely you are very young to be going out to work? If you'll excuse me for being curious – is this the first time you've done this sort of thing?"

Ilita nodded her head.

"I have just come from school, and as I do not know really what is expected of me, it may make the lady who is employing me very angry."

She could not repress the tremor in her voice, and she saw Mrs. Lynton's eyes soften as she said:

"Now don't worry yourself, dear. I'm sure you'll be all right as you grow accustomed, so to speak, to what's required."

She paused before she added:

"Her Ladyship's not herself, and that's the truth, ever since her accident. She was a great beauty, acclaimed everywhere she went, and even the Prince of Wales said she was the loveliest woman he had ever seen. So you can understand, Miss Marsh, what it's meant to her to be blind."

"Yes, of course," Ilita said, "and I will try to help her."

"That is what I'm sure you'll do, and if you read to her, it'll perhaps take her mind off herself."

Mrs. Lynton paused for a moment. Then she said:

"I think perhaps I should take you in to see Her Ladyship now. Suppose you take off your bonnet and cape and wash your hands after your journey? While you are doing that I'll ask if Her Ladyship'll be ready to receive you."

She went from the room as she spoke and Ilita, feeling as if she had been ordered about by a kind Nanny, or was being looked after by one of the Nuns, obediently took off her bonnet and tidied her hair.

Then she washed her hands in the cold water which she suspected had stood in the jug for a long time, but at least it took away the grime from the train.

In a way she felt it was a relief that her future employer could not see her and therefore would not criticise her face as her aunt would have done.

She would also not see that her gown was somewhat creased from the journey and, because she had worn it for a long time, was a little too tight over her breasts.

But before she had time to worry about herself Mrs. Lynton returned.

"I've brought Her Ladyship's maid to meet you, Miss Marsh," she said. "This is Miss Jones, and she thinks it'd be convenient for you to see Her Ladyship immediately."

Ilita held out her hand, but the lady's-maid seemed only to touch it with two fingers as she said:

"I'm not sayin' Her Ladyship'll not regret having asked for a reader now she's come! If you ask me, it's quite unnecessary and, as I've told Her Ladyship over and over again, if she wants anything read to her, I'm there to do it!"

As she spoke, Ilita could not help thinking that the maid's rather hard, uneducated voice would not be very agreeable to anyone who was blind, but she said quickly:

"Oh, please, I do hope I shall not be a trouble to you, but it would be very kind if you could help me. I have never been a reader before, and I know that I shall make a lot of mistakes."

"Whatever made you choose such a stupid sort of job?" Jones asked aggressively.

"It was not my choice," Ilita said, "and actually there does not seem to be anything else I can do."

"I thought you could sew!" Jones said almost rudely.

"Oh, I can do that," Ilita replied, "and I would love to help you with Her Ladyship's things, if you will let me."

For a moment Jones looked surprised, then she said grudgingly:

"Well, I could certainly do with a helping hand considering how much is expected of me."

Then as if she did not wish to be over-conciliatory she said:

"Come along now! Her Ladyship's waiting."

She walked across the corridor and Ilita followed her as she opened a high mahogany door.

It led into a bedroom which Ilita saw at a glance was extremely untidy.

It was a beautiful room with a canopied bed on a raised dias. There were three large windows on one side of it, opening, she suspected, on the front of the house.

While she was vividly aware of somebody lying back against a pile of lace-trimmed pillows in the bed, she also could not help seeing that there were clothes left lying untidily on the chairs and sofa.

There was also a miscellaneous collection of brushes, combs, and bottle of cream on the dressing-table and, just as the Marquis had noticed downstairs, there was no fire in the grate but the ashes had not been removed.

There was only time to for a quick glance, however, before a querulous voice from the bed asked:

"Is she here, this reader the Countess of Darrington sent me?"

Ilita walked nearer to the bed.

"Yes, Your Ladyship, I am here," she said, "and it is very kind of you to have me."

She would have dropped a curtsy if she had not thought

it unnecessary, since the woman in the bed had a bandage over her eyes.

Nevertheless, Ilita could see that she was very beautiful.

She had dark, almost black hair which hung over her shoulders and would have been most impressive if it had not been so untidy and obviously in need of a brushing.

Her skin was nearly white and her features classical enough to have been those of a Greek statue.

She was wearing a diaphanous nightgown which Ilita felt was almost embarrassingly low and transparent.

Then she saw to her consternation that the lace on the nightgown needed mending and it did not, in fact, look very clean.

The same applied to her sheets which, although they were edged with priceless Viennese lace, were spotted with food and had obviously not been changed for some time.

"God knows whether I shall find any help from a reader," The Marchioness said. "What I need are my own eyes with which to see, not yours!"

"At the same time, I am sure it will help you," Ilita said in her soft voice, "if I read things of interest in the newspapers, or perhaps one of the books which are being published week after week."

"I have not read any books since I was at school," the Marchioness said, "and that was a long time ago. And why should I want to hear what other people can enjoy, while I have to lie here in misery? Do you hear me – misery!"

"I am so sorry for you," Ilita said, "but I am sure things will get better. In fact, I know they will!"

The last words had come spontaneously to her lips, and she knew they were not what she thought she ought to say, but simply had been spoken despite herself.

The Marchioness stiffened.

"Why should you say that?" she asked. "How can you sound so certain that I shall see again?"

'I am sure," Ilita replied, "I am sure you will be able to see, although it may take a little time."

"Who told you to say that to me?" the Marchioness asked sharply. "All the doctors, all the Specialists have said they cannot be sure there will be any improvement. How can you be so certain about it?"

There was silence. Then Ilita said:

"Sometimes, just occasionally in my life, I have known things perceptively, as one might say by instinct, and not at all as a result of using logic or common sense. Perhaps I am doing something wrong in saying this to you, My Lady, but somehow I know in my heart that one day you will again have the use of your eyes."

Even as she spoke Ilita thought perhaps she was making a mistake and was raising the Marchioness's hopes unavailingly.

Then she knew that what she was saying had come from inside herself, and it was not wrong, but right that she should follow her instincts, rather than be afraid to do anything out of the ordinary.

"If that is true," the Marchioness said in a low voice, "then it would be the most wonderful thing that could happen! Do you hear, Jones? Do you hear what this young woman has said to me?"

"I hears, M'Lady," Jones said, "but she's not an Eye-Specialist, and it's no use your getting yourself all worked up for nothing."

"It is not for nothing," the Marchioness said. "If she is right – and why should she not be? – then I shall be myself again. That is all I want – to be as I was before that damned horse threw me! Oh, God, how could it have happened?"

She uttered a cry that was like one of agony, and instinctively Ilita put out her hand to lay it on the Marchioness's.

"Just believe," she said. "Faith is much more important than anything a doctor can give you."

She was thinking as she spoke of the faith that she had seen in operation when travelling with her father in the desert.

When the Arabs believed something would happen, strangely it did.

She had seen men who had been given up for dead recover from their wounds and live again. She had seen women who almost died in childbirth, live because they believed their other children needed them.

She knew Witch-Doctors could work miracles where the Medical Missionaries admitted they were helpless.

"Believe!" she said now in an insistent little voice. "Believe and I will help you."

The Marchioness's hand closed over hers, then she said:

"If you do that, I swear to you that I will do anything to show my gratitude – anything!"

Ilita could feel the Marchioness's fingers tighten on hers as if she was clinging to a life-line.

Then, because she was jealous, Jones broke in to say sharply:

"Well, I for one certainly hopes that what we're hearing isn't just a 'flash in the pan', so to speak. It's easy enough to talk, but what one wants to see is action."

"What I want to see is light, not darkness," the Marchioness murmured.

She released Ilita's hand, and Jones said:

"Your luncheon'll be coming up in a moment, M'Lady, and the best thing you can do is try to eat for a change."

Ilita looked enquiringly at the lady's-maid who said:

"You can leave Her Ladyship to me. She doesn't want people watching her while she's eating, and who shall blame her for that?"

Ilita walked to the door.

"Come back and see me later," the Marchioness said, "I want to talk to you."

"Very well, My Lady," Ilita replied.

She found, as she expected, Mrs. Lynton in the corridor and she had the idea that the door had been ajar and she had heard everything that had been said.

She did not speak, but walked into Ilita's bedroom, saying as she did so:

"I've been thinking, Miss Marsh, it would be best for you to have your meals up here. I know you will understand when I say that I don't think you'll fit in in the

Housekeeper's room, and of course not in the Servants' Hall. Therefore it would be best for your own sake and for everybody else's if you were to eat alone."

"Thank you, Mrs. Lynton, that is what I prefer."

"I'll see that one of the footmen brings you your luncheon, and if there's anything you want particularly, or do not like, you must tell me. After today, things'll be getting back to normal. And not before time!"

She spoke the last words with asperity as she walked out of the room, shutting the door behind her.

Ilita went through the communicating door into the Sitting-Room, thinking as she did so how strange everything had been and not in the least what she had expected.

Now she questioned herself as to how she knew the Marchioness would regain her sight and how she had been so positive in telling her so.

"It must have been you, Papa," she said to her father. "You told me what to say."

She knew he would understand, and so would her mother, that it was not what she consciously thought, but what she felt, and that was indisputable.

At the same time, when she was eating the luncheon that was brought to her on a tray by a rather nervous footman who waited on her somewhat awkwardly, Ilita was trying to piece together the strange things that had happened since her arrival.

She wondered if anybody would tell her what had happened in the house and how it got into the state it had just because the Marchioness had been stricken with blindness.

Her mother had often told her how great houses like Darrington House, and of course the same would have applied to Lyss Castle, ran like clockwork largely because most of the servants had been there all their lives.

They looked on it as their home and in a way as much theirs as the real owner's.

"They look upon it as if they really own it themselves," her mother had explained. "I know the servants in my home always talked of it as 'ours' not 'yours' and they would say:

" 'We are having a good season this year' or We are having a bad one', and it meant as much to them as it did to my father."

She had always explained to Ilita how in each department they trained over the years until they reached the top.

The knife-boy would become the pantry-boy, the pantry-boy would become a footman, first, second, third, until he became the sixth. Then when there was a vacancy he would become a Butler.

The same applied to the house-maids, the grooms and in all the various departments on the estate, such as the stone-masons, the carpenters, the laundry, the gardeners, the foresters and the keepers.

Each great house was a sort of State within a State, and Ilita, sitting in a hot oasis, the palm trees hardly moving in the warm breeze, found it more fascinating to listen to than a Fairy-Story, and asked her mother over and over again questions that belonged to her past.

But now, for some reason she could not understand, in Lyss Castle the machine had broken down and the people who should be turning the wheels had been sacked. It seemed to be all because their master the Marquis had not been there.

Why had he gone away?

It was all very interesting and rather like a mystery tale to which on the last page she would find the answer.

Once Ilita had eaten her luncheon she thought the first thing she would like to do before anything else was to explore the Castle.

Then she reminded herself that she was paid to be in attendance on the Marchioness and should find out, presumably from the somewhat antagonistic lady's-maid, at what time she would be required.

But having no idea how to get in touch with Jones, she opened the door leading out into the corridor to see if by any chance she was outside.

There was no sign of her, while the door into the Marchioness's room was tightly closed, and Ilita stood irresolute wondering what she should do.

Then there was a movement at the end of the passage and she saw walking towards her purposefully, and in a manner which told her instinctively that he was angry, the Marquis.

Chapter Four

As the Marquis reached her, Ilita realised he was looking angrier and more frightening than he had before.

She looked at him wide-eyed, wishing she could move away, but having no idea how to do so.

"I wish to speak to Her Ladyship," he said abruptly. "ask if she is ready to see me."

It was an order and Ilita walked towards the Marchioness's room, knocked gently on the door and opened it.

As she did so the Marchioness cried out:

"I want Miss Marsh! Is that you, Miss Marsh?"

"Yes, it is me," Ilita replied.

Because the Marchioness's voice sounded so urgent, she ran across to the bed leaving the door open.

The Marchioness put out her hand and she slipped hers into it.

"Tell me," she said instinctively, "tell me truthfully. Did you really say I would regain my sight?"

"Yes, I said it."

As Ilita spoke, she was aware that the Marquis had walked into the room and was now standing at the end of the bed.

Still with her hand held by the Marchioness, Ilita said:

"We will talk about that later, My Lady, but now His Lordship is here and wants to speak to you."

"I certainly do!" the Marquis said harshly. "Perhaps you would explain to me how you dared to give the order for my horses to be destroyed?"

His voice seemed to ring out with an anger that vibrated through the room, and the Marchioness, still holding on to Ilita, answered:

"Rufus threw me! That is why I am here, blind and helpless."

"So you decided to avenge yourself on all the others!" the Marquis said. "Fortunately Abbey was not so foolish as to obey you, and with the exception of Rufus they are alive. I could not have believed that anyone could be so cruel, so vindictive, as to behave as you have not only to the horses but to the whole estate!"

"So it had upset you, has it?" the Marchioness retorted. "Well, who cares? What use is this place to me now that I cannot see it?"

"It does not surprise me that you think of nobody but yourself," the Marquis replied. "You always have. When you tricked my father into settling all his money on you, he could never have imagined that you would behave in such a despicable and criminal manner towards the place that has been enshrined in the hearts of my family for generations."

"That is the right word," The Marchioness retorted. "Enshrined! You worship bricks and mortar, buildings and fields! What do you care that I am lying here dead, except that I am still breathing!"

Her voice rose until it was a shriek and the Marquis said coldly:

"That is a ridiculous way to talk, as you are well aware. I have sacked that drunken fool who was supposed to manage the estate for you, and now I ask you to give me a Power of Attorney to try and save something from the wreckage of what was once a place of happiness and prosperity."

"Give you Power of Attorney?" the Marchioness screamed. "I would rather give it to the Devil himself. I hate you, Terill, do you hear? I hate you and I always have. You tried to prevent your father from marrying me and now you and your rotten house, and your decrepit old servants can all go and drown yourselves as far as I am concerned!"

She paused for a breath before she said, shouting the words across the bed:

"Not one penny piece will I give you of the money your father gave me. It is mine, you do hear? – it is mine! If you and everybody else in this house were starving so much the better! I only wish I could see you and laugh!"

"If that is your last word," the Marquis said coldly, and now his voice was like a whiplash, "I can only say that your fall from the horse you had destroyed has affected not only your eyes, but your brain. You are mad, and the sooner I have you committed to an Asylum, the better!"

With that he turned and walked from the bedroom, slamming the door behind him.

In all this exchange Ilita had been unable to move, first because the Marchioness was still clinging to her hand, and secondly because she felt frozen into immobility by the violence of the animosity that flashed between the two people concerned like shafts of lightning.

Never had she heard anybody speak with such venom and violence, and she felt that every word they said to each other was almost like a blow inflicted on herself.

Then as the sound of the Marquis's footsteps echoing down the corridor died away she realised she was trembling.

"What does he mean that I am mad?" the Marchioness asked in a low voice. "Am I mad? And if I am, it is not surprising!"

"His Lordship is very angry," Ilita said in a small voice. "What can have happened to make him so incensed?"

The Marchioness sat up abruptly against her pillows.

"I will tell you what has made him angry," she said, releasing Ilita's hand for the first time. "It is because I hold the purse-strings! I, the stepmother he did not want, the woman he begged his father not to marry!"

She spoke with a relish that made what she was saying sound very unpleasant, and Ilita longed to get away and not be involved.

Yet she knew she must try to understand what was happening, though at the moment she felt utterly bewildered.

"The Marquis is your stepson?" she said after a moment's pause. "I . . I thought he was your . . husband!"

The Marchioness laughed, and it was not a pleasant sound.

"Terill would no more marry me than espouse the Witch of Endor," she said. "He hated me from the first moment his father found me, as every other man did, attractive."

There was a little silence, as if she was looking back to the days that were passed, then she said:

"I might have been too young for the fifty-year-old Marquis of Lyss, but why should I refuse such an advantageous marriage? I had no suitor who was more distinguished or more important socially."

Her voice softened as she added:

"I was very beautiful, very, very beautiful, Miss Marsh. There was no man in London who was not ready to fall at my feet, except of course for my stepson!"

She spat out the last words, then defiantly she added:

"But I have won! I have humbled him into coming to me for help, and now there is nothing he can do but watch the place and everything in it crumble to dust and ruins!"

There was so much satisfaction in the Marchioness's voice that it made Ilita shiver.

Then, hesitatingly, because she was frightened of upsetting her, she said:

"And when everything is in ruins . . will that . . make you . . happy?"

"Happy? What do I want of happiness now?" the Marchioness asked. "How can I be happy when I cannot see? At least if I am miserable, I will make everybody else miserable too."

Without thinking, Ilita gave a little cry.

"No, no! You must not talk like that!" she said. "It is wrong! It will hurt not only the people you are trying to punish, but yourself."

There was silence. Then the Marchioness asked:

"How can it hurt me more than I am hurt already?"

As if the words were put into her lips Ilita replied:

"What you are feeling and planning is a weapon which can turn against you. If you hate, your hatred poisons your whole being, while to regain your sight you must be whole and well both in body and in mind."

The Marchioness threw herself back against the pillows, and as she did not speak Ilita was afraid she was angry and that she would dismiss her immediately for being impertinent and interfering in a matter which had nothing to do with her.

The silence lasted for so long that at last Ilita said in a trembling voice:

"Shall I leave you alone, My Lady? Perhaps you would like to be alone."

"No, no, of course not," the Marchioness answered. "I want you with me. You are not to go away. I am only trying to understand what you have just said to me. You told me that you were sure I would regain my sight. Have you now changed your mind? Or are you admitting it was a lie?"

"It was the truth as I felt it," Ilita said, "but I know that hatred, anger and violence can prevent the body from healing. For your eyes to be healed, which is what has to happen, you must not inhibit the work of God by using the weapons of . . Satan!"

Once again as she felt the words come to her lips, she knew she was in fact stepping back into the past and quoting the sort of things she had heard so often from the wise women or the Elders in an Arab village.

It was the way they talked of their powers, and her mother had often said that there was a lot everybody could gain by learning from them.

"They are so fundamental about it," she said once to her daughter, "they see things perhaps more clearly than we do in what we call the 'civilised world'. Things for them are either black or white, good or bad, and a man either follows Allah or is against Him. There are no half measures!"

The Marchioness was very still after Ilita had spoken. Then she put out her hand gropingly until she found Ilita's and said:

"Help me! You have to help me! No one has ever given me even a ray of hope."

"It is there," Ilita said quietly, "like a light shining in the darkness, but you will have to find it for yourself."

As she spoke she looked around the untidy bedroom and at the Marchioness's torn nightgown and her hair falling over her shoulders unbrushed, and she said impulsively:

"May I suggest something to you, My Lady?"

"What is it?" the Marchioness asked.

"I think you would feel happier and more comfortable if the bedlinen was changed and the room was tidied. Perhaps while that was done you could move somewhere else."

"What does it matter what it looks like when I cannot see it?" the Marchioness argued. "I do not want to be fussed. I just want to lie here and wish I could die."

"That is not true," Ilita said impulsively. "You are wishing you could see and I would not like you to see at the moment the ugliness of your surroundings."

Now there was a silence of sheer astonishment before the Marchioness said:

"Are you saying that my bedroom, which I designed myself, is ugly?"

"It is very untidy and badly needs cleaning!" Ilita said firmly.

"And what do *I* look like?"

For a moment Ilita felt she had gone too far.

There was a note in the Marchioness's voice which she felt was one of warning, and she had a memory of her aunt telling her that if she lost her job it would be no use her coming back to her whining for another reference.

Then with a faint smile which the Marchioness could not see she replied:

"I would prefer, My Lady, not to answer that question."

The Marchioness gave a scream.

"That means I look ugly! What has happened to my face apart from my eyes? Is my skin blemished? Are there lines round my mouth and across my forehead? Tell me! Tell me the truth!"

"Does Your Ladyship really want to hear the truth?" Ilita asked softly.

"I order you to tell me what you really think!"

"You may be angry."

"What does it matter to you if I am angry?"

"Perhaps you would frighten me and then send me away."

"Do not be so ridiculous!" the Marchioness retorted. "Of course I am not going to send you away. You have to help me regain my sight. Now answer me – what do I look like?"

"I think," Ilita said quietly, "that you are the most beautiful person I have ever seen, but at the moment it is like looking at a picture that has been damaged or a statue of a Greek goddess that has been left out in a storm."

The Marchioness drew in her breath. Then unexpectedly she laughed.

"You are being very discreet, Miss Marsh," she said, "but I have got the message! Help me out of bed, and tell the housemaids to do what you want them to do with the room."

*　　　*　　　*

Nearly three hours later Ilita, feeling as if she had been battered about in a rough sea, left the Marchioness's bedroom.

She had taken her to the *Boudoir* next door which was in very much the same state as her bedroom had been, while she sent a message by the housemaid, who came to answer the bell, that she wanted Mrs. Lynton.

There was no need to explain to Mrs. Lynton what was required.

She took one look at the bedroom and the mess it was in and started to give curt orders to the housemaids who were obviously apprehensive that they would be blamed for its condition; the same condition that was to be found everywhere else in the great house.

Leaving Mrs. Lynton in charge, Ilita then hurried back to the Marchioness, who wanted to talk only of herself and her eyes and be assured and re-assured over and over again monotonously that Ilita was certain her sight would be restored to her.

It was difficult in the circumstances for Ilita not to question her own intuition and with the Marchioness sitting beside her, her eyes bandaged, unable to think or speak of anything else, it was impossible not to have doubts.

And yet, because she felt her father was guiding her in the extraordinary circumstances in which she found herself and which were so unlike anything she could possibly have anticipated, she was sure that she was doing and saying the right thing.

"It is willpower that matters most," both her father and mother had said to her at some time or another.

She remembered when she was quite small being told the story of an Arab Princess who just before she was to marry a famous and powerful Sultan had been stricken with one of the terrible eye diseases which were so prevalent in the East.

The Medicine Men, the Sooth-Sayers and the Astrologers had all said her condition was hopeless and there was nothing that could be done.

But she had a dream in which her eyes were washed in the clear water of a cascade and when she awoke she knew that was what she must find.

The tribe to which she belonged was situated in the very centre of one of the most isolated and waterless deserts in the whole of Africa.

The Princess set out alone, without attendants, without any directions, to find the cascade which her dream had told her would heal her sight.

It was a long story which took hours in the telling of the Princess wandering blindly and apparently aimlessly, existing only on the food she could find amongst the plants and shrubs growing in the sand.

Finally when she was so thin that she was little more than a skeleton, she found after months of wandering the cascade of which she had dreamt.

She heard the sound of it ahead of her, and feeling her whole being reaching out to it, she ran forward and flung herself into the water.

She was saved from drowning by some kindly native women who had been washing their clothes on the flat stones at the bottom of the cascade.

They gave her food and shelter and every day because she demanded it of them they led her back to the cascade.

After a week she could see the water indistinctly, and eventually as she washed her eyes the healing power of the water enabled her to see as clearly as she could before the disease had afflicted her.

Ilita had heard the story told many times in Arabic, and now as she related it in English to the Marchioness she felt as if her father and mother were close to her; as if they were sitting cross-legged on a sandy floor and had just finished consuming the feast of a whole sheep that had been slaughtered and roasted in their honour by an Arab Chieftain.

"Water?" the Marchioness said as the story came to an end. "Do you think water will help my eyes?"

"I think cold water might help, My lady," Ilita replied, "and also sunshine and air. Do you need to wear that bandage?"

"I wear it because I cannot bear to think of my eyes cold and vacant, staring at people like a Zombie!" the Marchioness snapped.

"Let us take it off," Ilita said gently. "I am sure it is a mistake to hide your eyes and to constrain them in any way."

The Marchioness removed the bandage and when she had done so, Ilita realised she had been quite right in thinking she was the most beautiful woman she had ever seen.

She was aware now that the Marchioness was much older than she had appeared at first. There were dark lines under her eyes and a few small wrinkles at the corners of her perfectly shaped lips.

At the same time she was beautiful, very beautiful, and Ilita said impulsively:

"I know now what is right for you and it is very important. You must think beauty, you must surround yourself with beauty, nothing that is not beautiful must come into your mind or your heart."

74

"That is a very big thing for your to ask of me," the Marchioness said. "I have lived with hatred for so long that I shall find it very difficult to change."

"But you must believe it would definitely prevent you from reaching the healing cascade as the Princess did, so you will be sensible and make your will obey you."

Again, unexpectedly, the Marchioness laughed.

"You are making me play a game," she said "Very well, Miss Marsh, I will play games with you. What do we do now?"

"When your bedroom is ready, I think you should rest for today," Ilita said. "But tomorrow you must get up, and as soon as you feel strong enough we will go out into the sunshine and walk. We will let the earth, the trees, the flowers, and of course the sunshine show you their healing powers."

"You are making it exciting for me," the Marchioness said, "but I do not want anybody to see me."

"When they do see you," Ilita said, "I promise you you will look as beautiful as before all this happened. But it has to be real beauty, not only outside, but in."

"I understand exactly what you are saying to me," the Marchioness said, "and at least it is something to think about, something to look forward to."

"Of course," Ilita agreed.

The door opened and Mrs. Lynton stood there.

"Your bedroom's ready, My Lady, if you'd like to return to it."

The Marchioness looked with a surprised expression on her face towards the door and Ilita knew she had not expected Mrs. Lynton to be there.

It was then that she remembered how the Housekeeper had told the Marquis she had been given her notice.

"It is Mrs. Lynton, is it not?" the Marchioness asked in a low voice.

"It is, M'Lady."

"I am glad you are back," the Marchioness said. "I did wrong to send you away."

For a moment Ilita knew it was difficult for Mrs. Lynton to answer her, then she said:

"Do not worry, Your Ladyship. I'll look after everything."

"Thank you, Mrs. Lynton," the Marchioness replied.

Ilita took hold of the Marchioness's arm and led her back to her bedroom where the elderly housemaid was waiting with a clean nightgown for her to put on.

But before she got into bed, at Mrs. Lynton's suggestion she sat down at the dressing table and allowed the maid to brush her hair.

There was no sign of Jones and Ilita did not like to ask questions. When the Marchioness was finally in bed and seemed rather tired, Mrs. Lynton suggested she should have a little sleep."

"After that, M'Lady," she said, "I'll see that your tea's sent up to you, and Miss Marsh can come back and talk to you."

"You will not go away?" the Marchioness said quickly to Ilita. "You will not disappear and I shall find I have dreamed you?"

"No, of course not!" Ilita replied. "As soon as you are ready for me, I will come back and talk to you."

The Marchioness slipped between the clean sheets and the bed looked very different from the way it had before.

Then as they watched her eyes with their long dark lashes drooping heavily because, suffering a natural reaction, she was in fact very tired, Mrs. Lynton and Ilita went from the room.

Outside in the passage Mrs. Lynton said:

"You've done a good job, Miss Marsh! I couldn't have believed that any Lady in this house should have been left in such a state. It's something that must never happen again!"

"I hope not," Ilita sighed.

Then she said a little nervously:

"I . . I am . . afraid Miss Jones will . . think I have . . interfered."

"Don't worry about Miss Jones," Mrs. Lynton replied, and her voice was sharp. "She's left!"

"Left?" Ilita exclaimed in astonishment.

"She realised I would force her to go anyway," Mrs. Lynton explained, "seeing the way she's neglected Her Ladyship, and as it happens she was ready to leave with Mr. Sheldon after His Lordship dismissed him."

- Ilita was listening wide-eyed as she added:

"They were too close, if you understand my meaning, Miss, and that's something that's not correct in a household such as this!"

Ilita felt there was nothing she could say and she was going to her bedroom when Mrs. Lynton added:

"His Lordship had asked to see you as soon as you are free. You'll find him in the Library. There'll be someone at the bottom of the stairs to show you the way."

Ilita looked at Mrs. Lynton apprehensively.

"He is still angry?"

"I have no idea," Mrs. Lynton replied, "but if he is, it'll not be with you. What he has found here has been a terrible shock, and it'll take His Lordship a little time to get over it."

Ilita could understand that. At the same time, she felt frightened as she went down the impressive gold and ebony staircase to the hall.

Now there were four footmen on duty, and they looked very different from the ones she had seen on her arrival.

She was led along a wide corridor and again there were huge mahogany doors with gold handles which were opened to admit her to the Library.

She went in feeling shy and conscious that, because there had been so much to do, she was still wearing the gown in which she had travelled from London.

It was an enormous Library with books reaching from floor to ceiling, and with long windows ornamented with the family coat-of-arms in the stained glass.

The Marquis was seated at a flat-topped desk.

He did not rise as she came towards him, and waited until she stood in front of him before he said:

"Now, Miss Marsh. I would like a truthful explanation of what you are doing here and who sent you."

It was not what Ilita had expected him to say and she replied:

"A friend of Her Ladyship recommended me as a reader, My Lord."

"I have been told that already!" The Marquis said sharply. "But I am not so stupid as not to realise that no ordinary reader would look like you, and no reader would manage to ingratiate herself so quickly and so competently with someone as difficult as my stepmother, unless they had some very good reasons for doing so."

"I . . I do not understand what . . you are . . saying."

"Then let me make it a little clearer," the Marquis said. "I suspect that knowing Her Ladyship is a very rich woman, you are looking, like a great many of your kind, for 'pickings'. Very well, tell me what you make of this engagement and I will consider whether it is worth retaining you or sending you away."

Ilita gave a little cry.

"Oh, please, My Lord," she said, "Let me stay! It is very, very important to me that I should stay here and not be . . dismissed! In fact, I do not think I have done anything wrong."

"You do not think it wrong to raise the hopes of a blind woman that she will see? Depending, of course, on how much she listens to you and how much she pays you for finding this miraculous cure!"

His voice was sarcastic and again Ilita gave a little cry.

"It is not like that at all!" she protested. "How can you think such a thing? Of course I am not trying to extract money from Her Ladyship! Why should I?"

She paused then she said:

"It is just that, almost as soon as she spoke to me, somehow I knew intuitively that her blindness was only temporary."

"How could you possibly know such a thing?" the Marquis demanded. "You are not a doctor, or are you one of those 'quack' Faith Healers?"

"It is impossible to explain, My Lord, but I can only say that I believe that one day, it may be a long time or a short, but the Marchioness will regain her sight."

"I have never heard such a lot of hocus-pocus," the Marquis said sharply. "You strain my credulity to breaking point, Miss Marsh, and all I can say is that I cannot believe a word of what is called 'clairvoyance'. You must have some reason for putting it over, and the obvious answer to that is money!"

Ilita's chin went up.

"That is very insulting, My Lord," she said, "and as I am not in a position to insult you, I think you are taking an unfair advantage!"

The Marquis raised his eyebrows.

"You are certainly very unexpected, Miss Marsh. How old are you?"

Without thinking, because she had not expected the question, Ilita told the truth.

"I am nearly nineteen."

"At such a young age," the Marquis said sarcastically, "you cannot expect me to believe that somebody has not rehearsed you very thoroughly in what you should say."

"No one has told me to say anything, My Lord. I was merely sent here by Her Ladyship's friend, and actually I only arrived in London yesterday."

"From where?"

Quickly Ilita thought perhaps she was being indiscreet and after a moment's obvious hesitation she replied:

"The . . country."

"In which part of the country do they teach Faith Healing, if that is what you are doing? Or instruct young women of your age to hoodwink eccentric women like my stepmother who, in my opinion, is mentally deranged?"

"That is not true!" Ilita said. "I can understand that you have been deeply hurt and upset by the condition in which you have found the house, but because the Marchioness is so beautiful it is perhaps more intolerable for her to be blind than for another woman who would have other interests besides herself."

"You are making excuses for her," the Marquis said bitterly. "Perhaps, as you are so clever, you can persuade her to change her mind and allow me to restore and preserve some parts of this house and its gardens."

"And, of course, the horses!" Ilita said almost to herself, feeling because she loved them that they were more important than anything else.

"Yes, the horses," the Marquis agreed. "Like human beings they need to be fed, and how am I to afford it when I have no money? How am I to pay the wages of the men who look after them? The same applies to the people in the house, the gardeners, the woodmen, in fact everybody on the estate which was once the pride of my father and my ancestors before him."

Ilita thought for a moment. Then she said:

"I would not wish to raise your hopes, My Lord, but I think I might be able to persuade the Marchioness to be a little more reasonable than she is at the moment. She has already promised me to try not to hate you and it would certainly help if you would cease to hate her."

As she finished speaking she realised that the Marquis was staring at her in astonishment.

"Who are you?" he asked, "and how can you, looking as you do, speak in such a way? What I do not understand is how, although you arrived only today and I found you sitting on the steps, it is possible that you have obtained such an ascendancy over my stepmother? Is it magic – black magic?"

Ilita laughed.

"White magic, My Lord, would be a better term, and quite frankly it is quite simple."

"Then I hope you will explain it to me," the Marquis said. "The doctors – and I imagine Her Ladyship has consulted the most important in the land, agree there is no cure and no hope for the future."

"Yet Hope and Faith is what everybody needs in life, whatever they are doing, whatever is happening to them," Ilita said.

She paused as if she was thinking out her argument in

the same way that she would have talked it over with her father, and she went on:

"It is hope that keeps an explorer struggling to the top of the mountain over trackless deserts to which there seems no end. It is hope which makes men fight and die for what they believe in, even though they know their cause is hopeless."

She gave a little sigh before she said:

"It must have been my father who told me what to say to Her Ladyship, and now that she has hope, I feel that things may be very different in the future."

She spoke quite simply and the Marquis threw himself back in his chair and exclaimed:

"I do not believe it! You are not real and this cannot be happening, not here in England at any rate."

There seemed no answer to this so Ilita said:

"I think, My Lord, if you no longer wish to talk to me, I should return. Mrs. Lynton is looking after Her Ladyship while I am away, but she has a great many other things to do."

"Very well, Miss Marsh," the Marquis said, "but I shall be watching you. I will be frank and say that although you are remarkably convincing, in fact almost suspiciously so, I am still not entirely persuaded you are exactly what you appear to be."

"What you are saying, My Lord, is that although you do not trust me, I may stay."

"As far as I am concerned," the Marquis conceded, "and if you can really improve the situation between Her Ladyship and myself, I shall of course be extremely grateful."

He looked at Ilita and then he said:

"It seems unbelievable that I should be talking like this to a complete stranger, and yet you have already seen and heard so much that you must have some idea of the position I am in. I am the owner of one of the most famous houses in the whole of Great Britain, with it and all its contents entailed on to me as the eldest son. But the revenue brought in by the estate is nothing like sufficient to maintain it properly, and the large additional income derived from other sources necessary to keep it up, was left by my father, persuaded by some means I do not like to think about, to his young wife for her life-time. Without this money, it is impossible for me to run this place, to pay the wages and carry out the repairs which are already overdue."

"I understand," Ilita said, "and it does seem a very strange situation. All I can say, My Lord, is that if I can help I will."

"Very well, Miss Marsh," the Marquis said. "I accept your assurance, and for the moment at any rate I think we can declare a truce. I will accept your explanation as to why you are here at its face value until it is proved that I am being hoodwinked."

Ilita gave a little curtsy.

"Thank you, My Lord, I am very grateful. I was so afraid when you sent for me that you intended to . . send me away."

"Why should that have worried you so much?" the Marquis asked.

"Because I have nowhere to go."

"How is that possible? You must have come from some-where and you could therefore return."

Ilita shook her head.

"It is not like that, but I do not want to talk about it. I want to stay here and know that I am safe."

She was afraid the Marquis might start to question her and once again she gave a little curtsy. Then as she walked towards the door her eyes were arrested by a picture which was standing propped up on a table in front of one of the bookcases.

For a moment she could not believe that what she was seeing was real, but it was indeed a very skilfully painted picture of some falls that she had visited with her father soon after her mother's death.

To Ilita it had always been the most beautiful scene she had ever known, and without thinking she stopped in front of the picture, taking in the shading of the dark outline of the rock and the rushing water falling hundreds of feet down into the basin of flat stones from which a mist rose iridescent in the sunshine.

For a moment she was transported back into the past and started when, without her realising he had moved from the desk, the Marquis said just behind her:

"I see you are admiring my picture. I do not suppose you have the slightest idea where it was painted?"

"At El Haufash on the edge of the desert," Ilita said automatically.

She spoke without thinking, and then she heard the Marquis say in a tone of utter astonishment:

"How could you possibly know that?"

"I always thought it was the most beautiful place I have ever seen," Ilita said. "I used to creep out very early in the morning while it was still dark and watch the sun come up over the horizon and see the first of its rays turn the water on the fall to gold. It was so lovely, but I felt I had stepped into a fairyland that I should never find again."

There was a long silence as if the Marquis was searching for words. Then he said:

"Are you telling me truthfully that you have actually been there?"

Ilita then awoke from a dream to remember she was supposed to come from a middle-class family who lived on the Darrington Estate.

It was too late now to retract what she had said, and she could only turn to look at the Marquis, her eyes large and frightened as she said:

"Yes, I have been there, but please . . please . . My Lord, will you . . forget what I have . . just said."

"Why should I do that?"

"For reasons I cannot tell you. But no one here must be . . aware I have been to . . Africa."

"Why?" the Marquis asked. "What is wrong, although it certainly is surprising to find that a woman of any age, let alone yours, has visited such a strange place?"

"That is so," Ilita said, "and that is why, please

promise me you will not mention it to the Marchioness or to . . anyone else!"

There was a desperate note in her voice and after a moment the Marquis said:

"Something has frightened you. You are really frightened."

"Yes, I am frightened," Ilita whispered, "and that is why I am throwing myself on your mercy and begging you to keep silent."

The Marquis made a gesture with his hands.

"In the circumstances how can I refuse?" he asked. "Do not worry, Miss Marsh. Your secret, although I find it extremely intriguing, is quite safe with me."

"Thank you . . thank you very much!" Ilita said breathlessly.

"But I hope," he said, "that you will come and look at this picture whenever you feel like it, and I have, as it happens, several more painted by the same artist when we were in Africa together."

"I would love to see them!" Ilita said. "It will be wonderful to bring back . . ."

She thought what she was about to say would be too revealing, and quickly, because she was more than a little agitated by what had happened, she said:

"Thank you, My Lord, thank you very much!"

She slipped from the room, even though as she reached the door he put out his hand to stop her.

Chapter Five

"I am frightened I shall fall," the Marchioness said.

"You are quite safe," Ilita answered. "Hold on to the banisters and I will hold on to you."

She paused before she said:

"Now just think how beautiful you look in that lovely chiffon dress walking down this magnificent staircase."

The Marchioness made a sound that was almost a laugh, and then step by step they descended very slowly into the Hall.

"Now you know where you are," Ilita said, as they walked towards the Drawing-Room, "and in a moment you are going to have a surprise."

Glover had hurried to open the door for them and the Marchioness, holding onto Ilita's arm, walked into the Drawing-Room.

She stopped still just inside the door and then exclaimed:

"It is lovely! I had no idea any flowers could smell so delicious."

Ilita laughed.

"The gardeners have brought in every rose and lily they could find," she said, "and everything else that had any scent."

"You have certainly been successful in making the room seem very beautiful even though I cannot see it," the Marchioness answered.

Ilita drew her towards the window where the sun was coming in like a golden haze.

Very gently she sat her down in a comfortable chair and said:

"Now I want you to imagine how lovely you look with the sunshine glittering on your jewels and the roses making a perfect background for your dark hair."

She nearly added that it was a pity that there was no one else to admire it. Then she remembered Mrs. Lynton had told her how the Marchioness, ever since she had been blind, had refused to see anyone.

"At first we had a great number of callers, Miss, as you can imagine," Mrs. Lynton had related. "But when they were always sent away, after a while they ceased coming and it's a pity if you ask me."

Ilita thought it was a pity too, but she did not know what she could do about it.

Over the past two days she had concentrated on gaining the Marchioness's confidence and trying to make her really believe that sooner or later her sight would return.

She had seen very little of the Marquis, but she had learnt that he was busy on the Estate and, according to Mrs. Lynton, deeply worried at how much there was to do and how deplorably everything had deteriorated since he had been away.

Ilita had not forgotten that she had promised to help him, but she was afraid of upsetting the Marchioness and causing her to behave again as she had done when she first found she was blind.

It was not only Mrs. Lynton who was willing to tell her what had occured, but the housemaids and Glover all had a tale to tell almost as if they were glad to have someone to listen to them.

"I really believes," Glover had said impressively, "that if 'Er Ladyship had had the strength, she would've pulled the Castle down brick by brick, she were that demented."

"I can understand her feelings," Ilita murmured.

"She went round smashing everything she could lay her hands on," Glover went on, "china and glass, and she would throw it on the floor or against the wall as if she wished to smash up the world."

Ilita could understand how frightened the household had been, especially as, in addition to her instinct for destruction, the Marchioness had sacked anyone who tried to control her or even those whom she met merely because they could see when she was unable to.

"Why did you not send for the Marquis?" Ilita asked Mrs. Lynton.

"That is what we wanted to do," Mrs. Lynton replied, "but when he heard the terms of his father's will, he was so incensed that he went off abroad to some outlandish part of the world. Africa I thinks it was."

Ilita, remembering the pictures in the Study, knew that was the truth.

She had longed to go back to see the other pictures the Marquis had promised to show her, but she had been afraid that if she did so, he would question her more closely as to why she had been in Africa and how she could recognise a place that he had thought was inaccessible to any woman.

At the same time she longed to see the pictures of the desert that brought back memories of her father, especially the Falls which, when she was at the Convent, had often been part of her dreams.

Now she opened a book that she had put out ready on the table by the chair in which the Marchioness was sitting and said:

"Today, because you look so beautiful and so very romantic, I am going to read you some of Lord Byron's poems. I want you to imagine you are living and moving in them yourself and that when he wrote them Lord Byron was thinking of you."

The Marchioness gave a little laugh.

"That would surely make me certain of my beauty! Do you really think I look beautiful? You are not just saying it to make me happy?"

"I swear to you on the Bible or on anything else you would like to suggest," Ilita assured her, "that you are the most beautiful person I have ever seen and now that you are smiling and looking so different from when I first met you, beauty is almost an inadequate word with which to describe you."

The Marchioness put out her hand to lay it on Ilita's arm.

"You are so kind to me," she said, "and I know that you think kindness is beautiful and unkindness is ugly."

"That is right," Ilita said as if she was teaching a child. "But now listen to this:

"She walks in beauty, like the night . . ."

She had only read the first line when the door opened and Glover said:

"Can I speak to you a moment, Miss Marsh?"

"Yes, of course," Ilita said.

She rose from the chair, putting down the book, and said to the Marchioness in a low voice:

"I think the staff are planning some special surprise for you. I will not be a moment."

She did not wait for the Marchioness to answer, but just hurried across the room and out into the Hall. Glover was just outside the door.

"I'm sorry to bother you, Miss," he said, "but Lord Grantham is here, and when he hears that 'Er Ladyship were downstairs he begged me almost on his knees to be allowed to see her."

"Who is Lord Grantham?" Ilita enquired.

Glover looked over his shoulder. Then he said:

"It was no secret that he loved 'Er Ladyship even before His Lordship died. As he lives in the Park, they saw a lot of each other."

"Then I suppose after Her Ladyship became blind she refused to see him," Ilita said.

"That's right, Miss. He were turned away until he came no more. He's here this morning because he learnt 'Is Lordship's back, and I understand the roof of the Manor House where he lives has fallen in and he doesn't know what to do about it."

Ilita drew in her breath. Then an idea came to her which seemed outrageous, though at the same time she knew that it might just work.

Quickly she made up her mind and said to Glover:

"Wait a few minutes and then ask Lord Grantham to go into the Drawing-Room. Do not announce him. Just allow him to walk in."

Glover looked at her with a knowing expression in his eyes and he said:

"I'll do what you says, Miss, even if I lose my head for disobeying 'Er Ladyship's instructions."

Ilita smiled at him and went back into the Drawing-Room.

She picked up the book of poems where she had left it, and without making any explanation continued to read the poem she had just begun.

She had just finished when the door opened and a man came into the room.

He was tall and good looking, although Ilita saw there were touches of grey at his temples. She guessed him to be about forty.

He stood for a moment just staring down the room at the Marchioness, and then as he walked resolutely towards her she realised someone was there and, looking up, she asked:

"Is that you, Terill?"

Lord Grantham did not reply. He moved steadily forward until he was standing beside the Marchioness.

Then he said in a deep voice:

"How can you be so beautiful, Esmé? Even more beautiful than I remembered."

The Marchioness gave a cry of horror.

"Gerald! It is you! You have no right to be here! Go away. I do not wish you to see me!"

"How can you be so cruel and so unkind as to forbid me to look at someone as beautiful as the sun, as perfect as the flowers, and as cruelly out of reach as the moon?"

"I do not want – anyone to – see me," the Marchioness said in a low voice.

"Why not, when you look just as lovely, if not lovelier than I remember you," Lord Grantham said.

As he was talking, Ilita, slowly on tip-toe, moved away towards the door.

Her heart had been beating apprehensively in case the Marchioness flew into a rage at his coming into the Drawing-Room.

But now as Lord Grantham sat down beside her and took her hands in his and raised them to his lips, there was a faint smile on the Marchioness's lovely face, and although she looked away from him she did not order him to leave.

Ilita reached the door and opened it silently.

"I love you, Esmé. I love you as I always have," she heard Lord Grantham say passionately, "and I want to look after you and protect you. How can you shut me out?"

Ilita closed the door and for a moment, out of sheer relief that things had not gone wrong, leant back against it.

Then almost involuntarily she made her own way down the corridor to the Library so that she could see the picture of the falls.

It was still standing where she had last seen it, and beside it, propped up on boards since they were as yet unframed, were two other pictures by the same artist.

One was of the desert at sunset and the other of an oasis with palm trees blowing in the wind with an Arab sitting huddled beneath them, his burnous pulled over his head as if to keep out the drifting sand.

The scenes were so vividly a part of the life she had led and so intrinsically a part of her memories that, staring at them, she stepped back in time to the happiness of a child who was safe with those she loved and had no fear of the future.

She was concentrating so intensely on what she was seeing that she did not hear the Marquis come into the room until he said just behind her:

"I thought you would find your way back here sooner or later."

"They are so beautiful," Ilita said, "and looking at them makes me feel homesick."

"You can hardly expect me to believe that your home is in Africa."

"It was once."

She could hear the regret and yearning in her own voice as she spoke.

"Tell me about it," the Marquis said quietly.

She then knew she had made a mistake.

She turned round so that she had her back to the pictures, and facing him said:

"I really came to look for you, My Lord."

"Why? What has happened?" he asked.

"Lord Grantham is here. He is with Her Ladyship, and he had really called because the roof of his house has fallen in."

The Marquis looked at Ilita as if he could not believe what she was telling him. Then he said:

"Can you really be thinking what I am?"

Ilita gave a little sigh.

"I thought perhaps, as I understand that Her Ladyship was very fond of Lord Grantham at one time, she would want to help him."

The Marquis stared at her and then walked to the fireplace to stand looking at her, with the pictures of the desert behind her, as if he could not believe what he saw.

Ilita looked at him enquiringly and after a moment he said:

"I am not now suspicious of you, Miss Marsh, so much as frightened! As I watch your mind working, I become more and more convinced that you cannot be a real person, but are someone out of a book."

He spoke quite seriously but Ilita laughed.

"If I came out of a book, perhaps I could go back into one! It would be a wonderful way to escape."

"Escape from what?"

She gave a little gesture with her hands.

"Anything that was frightening or unpleasant, and anything one did not want to do."

91

"What does that mean where you are concerned?"

"Nothing. Nothing at the moment," she said quickly. "I am very happy here and have everything I could possibly wish for. As I told Your Lordship before, all I want is to stay here and not be sent away."

"I am sure there is no danger of that at the moment," the Marquis said a little dryly.

Ilita glanced towards the door and then said:

"Perhaps Her Ladyship will be very angry with me for letting Lord Grantham see her."

"I think if she had been as angry as you fear," the Marquis said, "you would have learnt of it by now. Now what you and I must decide is how soon we join them and learn if, as we both hope, Lord Grantham has persuaded my stepmother to repair his roof."

"I am praying she will do that," Ilita said in a low voice. "I am praying very, very hard."

The Marquis looked at her sharply. Then he said:

"Why should it matter to you? You only came here three days ago. How can you possibly care what happens to Lyss Castle or to any of its inhabitants?"

She did not look at him or reply, and instead looked out of the long window to where she could see the huge trees in the Park with deer roaming beneath them.

"I suppose," she said, as if she was reasoning it out for herself, "I care because this is the first house I have lived in in England for so long that I had forgotten how beautiful my own country is. It is not only the grandeur of the Castle that appeals to me, it is the garden with its flowers, the lake with the yellow kingcups on its banks, and the feeling that, although I have not been here for so many years, it is where I belong."

The way she spoke was very moving and after a moment the Marquis said:

"Tell me why feeling as you do and, as you say, belonging here, you said the other day you would have nowhere to go to if you left Lyss."

His words were like a dash of cold water, and Ilita

remembered that she was not herself but someone called Marsh who had always lived in England and had no knowledge of any life except that of the countryside.

The fear was back in her eyes as she said:

"Once again, My Lord, I have spoken without . . thinking and ask you to . . forget what I have . . said."

"I am finding it very difficult," the Marquis said. "I like what you say and it interests me. There are a thousand questions I want to ask you, but I keep realising you are afraid and I find it very puzzling, at the same time frustrating."

"I am sorry," Ilita said quietly. "I think now I should go back to see if the Marchioness wants me. Perhaps in a few minutes you should come into the Drawing-Room to find out why Lord Grantham has called."

The Marquis laughed and it was a sound of genuine amusement.

"Are you really instructing me what to do," he said, "almost as if you were producing a play?"

He looked at her sharply and said:

"Is that what you are – an actress? Such an experienced and clever one that I am completely taken in by everything you say and everything you do!"

"That could be a compliment," Ilita said. "Actually Your Lordship must believe that I am nothing at all interesting, just someone who has come to your house unexpectedly to try in a very small way to help."

"I hardly think we could describe it as that," the Marquis said. "It is no small thing that after isolating herself from everybody and everything for nearly a year, my stepmother has come downstairs. Nor is it a small thing, Miss Marsh, as far as I am concerned, that you are trying to help me."

"I am trying. I promise you I am trying!" Ilita said.

She clasped her hands together with the intensity of her feelings and then the way the Marquis was looking at her suddenly made her feel shy.

She felt the colour come into her cheeks and turned

hastily to the door saying as she did so:

"I am sure we should go to the Drawing-Room."

"I suggest you go," the Marquis said, "and tell Grantham if he wishes to see me he can join me here."

Impulsively Ilita turned round and took a step towards him:

"No," she said. "I am sure that is wrong. I feel you should come to the Drawing-Room and let either your stepmother or Lord Grantham tell you what is wrong."

She paused and went on as she thought it out:

"If they do that it will be tantamount to asking you to repair the house. But as you cannot repair it without money, Her Ladyship will have to offer to help."

"I am following your reasoning, Miss Marsh," the Marquis said. "At the same time it astonishes me that at your age you should think out a plan so ingenious and at the same time so essentially human."

He smiled as he went on:

"But perhaps you yourself are not human, but a goddess from Olympus come down amongst mankind in a disguise to perplex and bewilder them."

"I thought there was enough here to bewilder you already before I arrived," Ilita said.

The Marquis smiled at the quickness of her reply.

Then feeling it was absurd for both of them to go on talking as if something very fundamental and important was not happening, he said:

"Go ahead. Let us get it over. If we fail I suppose there is always the chance that we may try again."

"I have the feeling that we will not fail," Ilita whispered in a very low voice.

"The same feeling that tells you my stepmother will see again?"

She nodded and then she said:

"I know you do not believe me, but I cannot help knowing it, almost as if I was hearing someone tell me what is happening."

"Then let us hope that 'someone' whoever 'he' may be,

is not mistaken," the Marquis said.

The way he spoke told Ilita that he was hoping against hope that she was right and he was also fighting the suspicion that he might be being hoodwinked.

Without saying any more she left the Library and hurried down the corridor to the Drawing-Room. As she went she found herself praying that her plan would come right, if only to confound the Marquis.

'He still thinks I am some sort of crook,' she thought, then wondered why it mattered so tremendously to her to prove him wrong.

Tentatively and very quietly she opened the Drawing-Room door.

There was no sound of voices and for a moment, with a pang of her heart, she thought Lord Grantham had already left.

Then she saw the Marchioness had moved from where she had been sitting so that Lord Grantham could be beside her on the sofa.

He had his arms around her and was kissing her passionately and demandingly while her hand was on his neck.

Very carefully, so that they could not hear her, Ilita shut the door. She then ran back as fast as her legs could carry her to the Library.

She burst in to find the Marquis standing in front of the fireplace where she had left him.

He turned his head towards her as she appeared, with a questioning look in his eyes. Without thinking Ilita ran towards him, too excited to think of anything but the success she had prayed for.

"It is all right! I am sure it is all right!" she said breathlessly. "Lord Grantham is kissing Her Ladyship. How then could she refuse him anything?"

Without meaning to she put out her hand to the Marquis, and having covered each of hers with his, he held them against his chest.

"Now I know," he said in a deep voice, "that you are a

witch! I might have expected it from the moment you arrived, except I had no idea that witches looked like you."

"I did not really cast a spell!" Ilita said. "I just did what seemed the natural thing to do."

"And very, very cleverly."

His fingers tightened on hers, and for the first time she realised how close they were together and that he was touching her.

Shyly she pulled her hands away and because she had no wish to meet the Marquis's eyes, she walked across the room to look out of the window at the Park.

"Perhaps thanks to you," the Marquis said after what seemed like a long silence, "everything can be restored to the perfection there was in the past."

"I prefer to think of it as stepping forward rather than back," Ilita said. "In the past there are always regrets when we have lost it. In the future there is hope, the hope that I am trying to give your stepmother."

"Who can say things like that at your age?" the Marquis said. "How can you attempt what you do? I am convinced, Miss Marsh, that if you do not answer my questions soon I will become demented."

Ilita gave a little laugh and turned to the window.

"That is something which must not happen, My Lord! In any case I have the feeling that soon you are going to be so busy that you will have no time to puzzle over my past and my problems."

"Now you are fishing for compliments," the Marquis said. "And if we are talking of the future, I too have a feeling that if you have planned to put your hand to the plough, you will have to carry on with the good work, however hard you may find it."

"That is what I want to do," Ilita said, "if only I can stay here."

They talked for another quarter of an hour, fencing with each other in words, Ilita feeling that all the time the Marquis was trying to catch her out, or trip her up, although she was always clever enough to elude him.

Finally, as they walked side by side to the Drawing-Room, Ilita's eyes were sparkling, and there was a flush of excitement in her cheeks, not only because of what was happening to the Marchioness but because she was finding it fascinating to be with a man who was so quick and intelligent.

She knew she had to convince the Marquis that she really was what she purported to be.

It was a situation she had never been in before, any more than she ever had the chance of talking to a man like the Marquis.

She found it fascinating, even while at times she was apprehensive that he might guess the truth, and in consequence she might be obliged to leave the Castle.

Not that she herself was of any importance whatsoever, as her aunt had been the first to tell her.

At the same time, the Darrington-Coombe family was highly respected and of considerable social consequence, and as a member of it she could not behave as could the obscure middle-class Miss Marsh.

"Whatever happens, they must never find out who I really am," she told herself.

She remembered how her aunt had threatened that if anyone did discover her identity she would put her into a Convent by force.

But at the moment she was thinking with joy not of herself, but of the Marchioness.

As she entered the Drawing-Room her heart leapt as she saw they were still sitting on the sofa, and now Lord Grantham was holding both the Marchioness's hands in his.

As they entered the room he rose slowly to his feet, and holding out his hand to the Marquis said:

"I came here to see you, Lyss, but I was fortunate enough in your absence to be entertained by your stepmother."

"We are delighted that today she is well enough to come downstairs," the Marquis said.

"Listen, Terill," the Marchioness said. "Poor Gerald is in trouble. His house has collapsed over his head, and if it rains the water will be pouring into his bedroom."

"That sounds very uncomfortable," the Marquis remarked, "but I am not sure what I can do about it."

"Do not be so ridiculous!" the Marchioness said. "Something must be done immediately! The only difficulty is, I am not certain who on the estate is left to cope with such a situation."

She spoke hesitatingly and the Marquis did not help her.

Then as the Marchioness waited, almost as if she was frightened of capitulating too easily, Ilita went to her side.

"I am sure Lord Grantham's house," she said quietly, "is very old and very beautiful, and he cannot lose or spoil anything so beautiful, can he?"

The Marchioness laid her hand over Ilita's as if she was well aware the word 'beautiful' had a particular significance for her.

Then she said, and she seemed almost to force the words from between her lips:

"Please, Terill, do what you can for Gerald, and while you are doing so, you had better take over the whole estate, as you wanted. I am too helpless to cope with it."

The Marquis drew in his breath, and it seemed to Ilita as if he squared his shoulders and became immeasurably taller. Then he said:

"You really mean that?"

"I mean it," the Marchioness said. "According to Gerald, and of course, Miss Marsh, it is far more important for me to sit about looking beautiful than to worry my head over broken roofs, rusting pipes, and dilapidated cottages."

"Of course it is!" Lord Grantham said. "Why should you think of anything that is not as lovely as yourself?"

"Thank you, Gerald."

Lord Grantham took the Marchioness's hand and raised it to his lips.

"I am promising myself," he said, "that as soon as the house is repaired I will be able to persuade you to be my first guest."

"Thank you!" the Marchioness said. "And perhaps by then I shall not only be able to hear what is being done, but see it."

Lord Grantham's fingers tightened on hers.

"I shall be praying that will happen," he said, and his voice was very sincere.

When he had gone, Ilita took the Marchioness upstairs because she was obviously tired.

Having been lying in bed for so long, she had found even a little physical exertion was exhausting and Ilita guessed she was also tired emotionally.

They did not talk about what had happened until she was back in bed. Then as she lay on the clean pillow-cases smelling of lavender she said:

"Gerald loves me! I am sure, Miss Marsh, that Love comes in your list of beautiful things."

"Love is the most important of them all!" Ilita said quickly. "For Beauty is Love, and Love is Beauty."

"So many men have loved me," the Marchioness said, "but I suppose, really, I have never loved them."

"You must try to give love as well as receive it," Ilita said, "and I am sure when you do, you will be even more beautiful than you are at the moment."

The Marchioness gave a little laugh of happiness.

"You and Gerald both make me feel that my eyes are unimportant, and that I can manage without them. That is not true, but I want to believe it."

"What you have to believe," Ilita said quietly, "is that because you are happy, because love is all around you, your eyes will be filled with it, and life will come back into them."

She talked to the Marchioness for a little longer, then as she fell asleep she left her with a housemaid within call if she should need her.

She walked downstairs, not really aware where she was

going, only feeling that everything was filled with sunshine and she need no longer be afraid.

The front door was open, and she walked out into the garden and down a path which led from the formal gardens with their yew hedges and flower-beds towards the wildness of the lake.

As she reached it, she found she was not the only person who had come to look at the beauty of the silver water with the swans moving serenely over it, and the irises and glowing yellow kingcups reflected in it.

Coming from between the shrubs she saw there was a man standing with his back to her, and she realised it was the Marquis.

She thought perhaps he wanted to be alone and she should go away from him. Then as she hesitated, it was too late.

He turned, and seeing her, held out his hand and drew her to the water's edge beside him.

For a moment he said nothing, but she was vividly conscious of the strength of his fingers and the nearness of him.

Then he said:

"How do you do it? How can you be so wonderful, so unbelievably fantastic, as to rescue me from what was a hell of hopelessness and depression and give me back something I thought I had lost completely?"

Ilita could not answer him because there were no words in which to do so.

Suddenly the Marquis put his fingers under her chin and turned her face up to his.

"What are you thinking about behind those ridiculously innocent eyes," he asked, "and that tiny childlike face that apparently holds all the wisdom of Solomon?"

"And what can I give you to express my gratitude?" he added.

She had a feeling that suspicion of her motive was underlying his words as when he had first spoken to her, and she said quickly:

"I . . I want nothing . . of course I want nothing! I am just relieved and happy that you can now do everything you want to do to make the Castle as beautiful as it ought to be!"

"Is that really the answer?" the Marquis enquired. "I am prepared to offer you half my Kingdom, or at least, shall we say, something very pretty and glittering which, if nothing else, will be a support to you in your old age."

Ilita moved quickly so that he could not retain his hold on her chin.

"Now you are spoiling everything!" she said. "It has all been like a Fairy Story, but you are making what I have done seem horrid . . and I do not want your presents, or your gratitude. I only want you to be happy."

"And why should you want that? After all, I am only a stranger," the Marquis said.

Ilita made a little gesture with her hands.

"Time is immaterial," she said. "One may know some-one for years and years, and yet they are still an enigma: still, one might say, out of reach. On the other hand, sometimes when one first meets a person one is sure one has known them for an eternity of time."

She spoke softly and was not aware that the Marquis had moved a few steps nearer to her until he said:

"Is that what you feel about me? Because as it happens, while I have struggled against it, it is what I feel about you."

As he spoke he pulled her into his arms and before she could be aware of what was happening, before she could even draw in her breath, his lips were on hers.

He kissed her gently, at the same time possessively.

Then as she felt the strange vibrations flow between them which was different from anything she had ever felt before, his arms tightened and his lips became more insistent, more demanding.

To Ilita it was so strange, so unexpected, that she felt as if the whole world had turned upside-down and the sky was swimming dizzily above her.

And yet at the same time she knew that, just as she had been vividly conscious of the Marquis from the very first moment she found him beside her on the steps and felt that he menaced her, so now he seemed to take possession of her so that she had no identity of her own and was no longer herself but his.

As if the Marquis felt the same, he raised his head and looked down at her for a moment as if he could hardly believe what he saw.

Then because Ilita could neither move nor speak, he was kissing her again, kissing her with long, slow passionate kisses that seemed to draw her heart from her body and time stood still.

Chapter Six

Because she felt shy the following day, Ilita took every precaution not to run into the Marquis.

After he had kissed her until she was breathless, dazed and bewildered by the wonder of it, she suddenly realised how reprehensible it was for her to be in such a position, and felt sure her mother would have disapproved.

At the same time, she knew the Marquis's kisses were the most wonderful thing she had ever known in her whole life, and it was what she dreamed of in her Fairy Stories when she was a child.

She had longed for them while she was at the Convent when the other girls talked of being married and how important their husbands must be.

What she wanted was love, the love she had seen between her father and mother, the love she knew was more precious, more perfect than any social significance.

How could coronets, titles or even money matter to her beside the fact that one's whole being responded to a man the moment he came into the room.

She had seen her mother's eyes light up so that her face became illuminated, as if her love transformed her.

That was the love Ilita knew she was feeling as the Marquis's lips held her captive and his arms encircled her so that she felt as if she need no longer be afraid.

Then she knew that because she loved him it would be very difficult when he questioned her again to refuse to tell him the truth and admit who she was.

If she did that she would have to leave.

It all flashed through her mind. At the same time her body quivered with such ecstasy that she felt she must be part of the divine and a rapture she had no idea existed upon the earth.

Then the Marquis had raised his head and said:

"How can you do this to me? How can you make me feel as I do about you?"

There were no words in which to answer him, and yet, because she realised the question of which she was so afraid would come next, she made an inarticulate little sound and, before he could prevent her, ran away.

She ran back from the lake through the garden and into the house, and only when she was in her bedroom did she throw herself down on the bed and hide her face in the pillow.

How could it have happened? How could anything so exquisite, so perfect have happened? It was the last thing she could have expected, being employed in a position which she knew ranked only as that of an upper servant.

It was then, because Ilita was very intelligent, that she faced the fact that even if the Marquis loved her as he said he did, there could be no question of their becoming husband and wife and being as happy as her father and mother had been.

Her mother had explained to her why her father had been so annoyed that she had married the penniless younger son of an Earl rather than accept the position he had planned for her as the wife of a distinguished Peer whose position at Court was unassailable.

"I cannot understand, Mama," Ilita has said, "why my grandfather was so angry. After all, Papa was an Honourable, and certainly a Gentleman."

Her mother had laughed.

"There is no doubt about that, darling, but you must understand that as there was no likelihood of Papa ever becoming the Earl of Darrington he was really of little consequence socially, and because your grandfather thought I was pretty he was very ambitious for me."

"Not pretty, Mama, beautiful!" Ilita corrected, and her mother replied:

"The only point for me of being beautiful was when I could see how much it meant to your father! How every time he told me how lovely he thought I was it thrilled me and made me feel as if I was flying in the clouds far above the earth!"

Her mother had spoken in a dreamy voice as if she was thinking back over the rapture that they had both felt when they were married against her family's wishes, but had known that the world was well lost for love.

"That is what I want," Ilita told herself now, but she knew the Marquis would be different.

He might kiss her, he might love her with all his heart and mind, but his brain would tell him clearly and distinctly that his wife must be of equal consequence to himself.

Therefore, he would never think of asking the middle-class Miss Marsh to be his wife and the Marchioness of Lyss.

It flashed through her mind that perhaps if she told him who she really was, it would make a difference.

Then she knew that a great many difficulties would arise from that: first the Marquis would undoubtedly be horrified that she was employed in a lowly position in his household; secondly, that she had stayed at the Castle unchaperoned would put her in a position that was unthinkable for the Marchioness of Lyss.

'I ought to go away,' Ilita thought.

Then she knew that every instinct of her body cried out at the thought of leaving the Marquis.

Moreover, she had nowhere to go, and certainly she could not return to ask the assistance of her aunt.

She knew only too well that the Countess had not been speaking idly when she said she would incarcerate her in a Convent from which she would never be able to escape.

"How could I bear it, how could I live out of the world and be confined by bare walls and a life of constant prayer?"

She lay on the bed for a long time before she sat up and

forced herself to try and think more clearly.

"What shall I do, Papa?" she asked, feeling her father must be near her and would understand the predicament in which she found herself.

Then, when finally she rose to go to her Sitting Room, she found a footman had just come up with her dinner.

It was impossible to eat very much of the delicious dishes which she guessed the Marquis was also eating alone downstairs in the Dining-Room.

Then when the footman removed the last course he said:

"His Lordship's compliments, Miss, and he asks if later, when Her Ladyship's retired for the night, if you're not too tired, you'll join him in the Library."

Ilita hesitated for a moment. Then she said:

"Will you thank His Lordship and say that as I am somewhat fatigued, I would like, unless of course it is a matter of urgency, to go to bed early."

"I'll tell His Lordship," the footman said.

When he left the room Ilita felt as if she was shutting herself out of Paradise, but she knew she was doing the right thing.

*   *   *

The following morning the Marchioness could talk of nothing but Lord Grantham, and spent hours preparing herself to receive him when he called on her at twelve o'clock as he had promised.

"I think by that time Terill will have inspected his house and decided what can be done to repair it," she said.

"I thought His Lordship was very charming," Ilita said tentatively, then added: "You must not think me impertinent, My Lady, if I ask if you are going to marry him."

The Marchioness gave a little cry.

"It is what he wants, it is what he has been begging me to do. But how, Miss Marsh, can I do such a thing when I am blind?"

"Would it matter very much if you were happy together?" Ilita asked softly.

"Of course it would matter!" the Marchioness replied. "How could I not be conscious every moment that I have to be led about like a dog? That I cannot eat in front of my husband because I could not bear him to see the mess I make? How could our marriage survive anything that was so sordid, or, as you would say, 'ugly'?"

"I do not think you are right," Ilita said slowly, "although I can understand how you feel."

"Of course you can, you are a woman too. But how could I be certain when with him my hair was not untidy, that there was no mark on my face or on my gown, and I did not look grotesque when I was reaching out to find something?"

"It seems so sad," Ilita said quietly, "when he loves you so much."

"If I could see," the Marchioness went on as if she was following her own thoughts, "I would make Terill do up the Dower House for us. It is very attractive and was built in the reign of Queen Anne. I have often imagined myself living there. It is certainly not as large and rambling as this Castle. In fact my husband used to say that the panelled rooms and the fine needlework of the curtains made a perfect background for my looks."

As she finished speaking the Marchioness gave a little cry and added:

"What is the point of talking about it! I am blind! Although you tell me that one day I will be able to see, how long will I have to wait?"

Ilita did not answer and the Marchioness went on:

"Suppose I regain my sight when I am old, wrinkled and grey? What would be the point of looking in the mirror at a hag-like creature whom no man will love?"

"Do not frighten yourself," Ilita said in her soft voice. "Just believe that everything will come right, your Fairy Story will come true and you will live in the Dower House."

She paused for a moment before she said:

"Papa told me once that one of the ways in which the

Arabs work their magic was to make a picture in their words of what they wanted, and see it with their 'inner eye' until their wish was fulfilled."

The Marchioness was listening and Ilita went on:

"See yourself in the Dower House, see yourself moving through its rooms putting the pictures straight, tidying the cushions, arranging the flowers. You are there, you are beautiful, and you can see!"

There was a little silence. Then the Marchioness said:

"You are making me believe it! Oh, God, it is what I want to happen!"

"Then picture it. See it clearly and believe it will come true," Ilita said.

The new lady's-maid whom Mrs. Lynton had appointed to replace Miss Jones came in to dress the Marchioness in one of her beautiful gowns.

Ilita then guided her down the stairs to where Lord Grantham was waiting for her, praying as she did so that what she had said to the Marchioness would happen.

She went upstairs again and found Mrs. Lynton waiting for her in her bedroom.

"I've a surprise for you, Miss Marsh," she said.

"What is it?"

"The seamstress has practically finished two of your gowns and she'd like, when you have a minute free, to fit them on."

Ilita gave a little cry of delight.

When the maids had first unpacked for her Mrs. Lynton had seen the rolls of muslin that Mrs. Fielding had given her in London, and Ilita had explained:

"When I came here I had only the clothes I had worn at school, but somebody who was very kind gave me these rolls of muslin which were originally intended for curtains."

"They are very fine quality," Mrs. Lynton said. "Do you intend to turn them into dresses?"

"As soon as I have the time," Ilita said. "I thought one of them would make an evening gown, although it is very unlikely I shall need one, and the other three would be for the day."

"There's no difficulty about that," Mrs. Lynton said. "There's a seamstress in the Castle and she tells me she's had a little or nothing to do since I ceased to be in authority."

"A seamstress?" Ilita exclaimed.

Then she remembered her mother telling her that when she was a girl there had been a seamstress in her grandfather's house who had not only made all their gowns, but mended the linen and repaired the curtains.

When Mrs. Lynton sent her to see Ilita she seemed a very old woman, but her eyes were sharp and she understood exactly what was wanted, promising to make the gowns as quickly as possible.

Now as she fitted them on with Mrs. Lynton watching, Ilita thought they were pretty enough to have come from any expensive Bond Street shop.

One of the gowns was of sprigged muslin, embroidered all over with tiny white flowers with a touch of green against a white background.

It made her look very young and at the same time ethereal, as if she had just stepped out of the flowering shrubs or from between the trunks of the leafy trees.

The ribbon, which Mrs. Fielding had also given her, was white, while for the evening gown made of muslin ornamented with pink roses which had been meant for the cot in the Nursery, there was a pink sash which fell down behind the full skirt like a cascade.

This gown had tiny puffed sleeves and a low décolletage.

Looking at her reflection in the mirror Ilita wondered if there would ever be a chance to wear it and for the Marquis to see her in it.

Then she told herself severely that she had to be sensible and not think about the Marquis or what had happened yesterday.

It was, however, impossible to prevent herself, as the

109

day passed, from sending her thoughts winging towards him.

She knew quite well that with the new authority which his stepmother had given him there were thousands of things for him to see to on the estate and dozens of people wanting to talk to him.

"He's not thinking of me," she told herself.

And yet she had the feeling it was impossible for either of them not to think of the other, for they were linked by some invisible vibration that was stronger than common sense or any direction of their brains.

"I must not see him! I must keep out of his way, otherwise I know he will continue to ask me about myself and will think it very strange when I can tell him nothing . . nothing!"

She repeated these words to herself over and over again, and when Lord Grantham returned in the afternoon, after the Marchioness had rested, to have tea with her, she was sure that the Marquis was waiting for her in his Library, puzzled that she did not join him there.

Ilita went upstairs and sat in her own Sitting-Room trying to reason out how they could continue as they were, or how she could persuade him into letting her stay on in the Castle as a quite unimportant reader to his stepmother.

The Marchioness, helped up the stairs by two footmen, was glowing with happiness as Ilita joined her in her bedroom.

"You have had a nice time?" she asked.

" 'Nice' is not the word for it!" the Marchioness answered. "I have been in Heaven after enduring a hell that no human should be made to suffer."

She obviously did not want to talk and Ilita therefore sent for the maid to help her undress.

"Gerald is coming to see me tomorrow," she said as she lay back against her pillows. "You will have to help me, Miss Marsh, to think of sensible arguments he will accept instead of pleading, begging, demanding that I marry him immediately!"

She gave a deep sigh.

"God knows, it is what I want, but it is something I dare not do, for his happiness as well as mine."

Ilita had already suggested that the Marchioness should eat as many green vegetables as possible, telling her that the Africans who lived near water always had stronger and healthier eyes than those who spent their time in the desert.

"I am sure too that honey is very helpful," she added.

Because the Marchioness was amenable to any suggestion, she ate honey with her breakfast in the morning, and had a spoonful of honey last thing at night before she went to sleep.

At the same time Ilita was aware that the fear, lest her hope of being able to see was just an illusion, was always in the back of her mind.

The Marchioness must know too that, because she was getting older, time was passing, and every day of blindness was a day wasted, a day that she could never regain.

Ilita felt they should leave no stone unturned and suggested that perhaps the Marchioness would like to see the Eye Specialists again who had attended her after the fall from the horse.

"What is the point?" the Marchioness asked. "They told me there was nothing they could do. They could not find any bones that were broken, and one doctor suggested it was a nervous affliction, while the other was quite certain it was a physical one."

She was silent for a moment. Then she said:

"I have no wish to see them, but only to trust you! Are you willing that one day I will open my eyes and see the world as I used to see it?"

"I am willing, praying and believing," Ilita said, and there was nothing she could add to that.

The Marchioness however was in a querulous mood

111

after Lord Grantham had left and refused at first to undress and go to bed.

Finally, when it was late and her dinner was getting cold, Ilita persuaded her to undress, get into bed and try the delicious dishes. But even then the Marchioness refused to rest.

"Read to me," she said. "Read so that I will think of other things. After all, that is what you came here for."

"Yes, of course," Ilita replied. "Shall we go on with Byron's poems, or would you like me to start a story that we can read every night?"

"I do not mind," the Marchioness said. "I just do not want to think, so read me anything you think will make me forget for a little while, at any rate, about myself."

Ilita fetched a book from the *Boudoir*, but it was growing late when the Marchioness's eyes closed at last and she fell into a restless sleep.

Ilita tip-toed out from the room and as she closed the door she found Mrs. Lynton outside.

"I wanted to help you, Miss Marsh," she said, "but I could not think of anything I could do."

"I think Her Ladyship is asleep now," Ilita replied.

"I'm afraid you've missed your dinner," Mrs. Lynton went on as Ilita opened the door to her Sitting-Room. "I've had it taken away to have something cold brought upstairs. I expect you're hungry."

"Not really."

"Everything's been at sixes and sevens!" Mrs. Lynton exclaimed. "His Lordship was expecting to dine in, then changed his mind and went out at the last moment. I should think the Chef is in a temper! If there's one thing he dislikes it's changes and cancellations! He's very proud of his food."

"As well he might be!" Ilita agreed. "It is always delicious!"

When finally she had eaten her dinner, she remembered Mrs. Lynton had said the Marquis had gone out, and thought that left her free to go downstairs to look at the pictures of the desert in the Library.

She had been longing to see them again, but had been half-afraid that in her determination to avoid the Marquis she would not be able to do so.

She slipped down the stairs, noticing there were two footmen on duty waiting for the Marquis's return.

She went into the Library, finding there were oil-lamps to light the room, but when she entered she gave a little cry of disappointment.

The pictures were not there.

She wondered where the Marquis had put them, and thought perhaps he had sent them away to be framed.

Then as she was wondering and thinking how sad it was not to see the cascade which had meant so much to her as a child, the door opened and the Marquis came in.

He was in evening dress and looking, she thought, extremely magnificent.

As soon as he appeared she realised she had been very foolish in not expecting, as it was growing late, that he would come home, and he might therefore think she had been deliberately waiting for him.

Quickly, because she was shy, she said:

"I . . I am sorry . . I did not mean to intrude . . I only came to see the pictures."

"I thought that was what you were doing when the footmen told me they had seen you go into the Library," the Marquis said. "I have a surprise for you, and I also want your opinion as to whether they are in the right place."

He led her out of the Library and down the passage where he opened the door of a room in which she had never been before.

It was a very pretty square room and the moment she entered it she understood why the three pictures of the desert were already framed and hung on one wall.

On the others there were pictures of exotic, strange animals, some by George Stubbs, some by artists that she did not know but who painted in the same original manner.

There were tigers, cheetahs and lions in the pictures, and

somehow the furnishings of the room seemed to blend in with them and with the pictures of the desert.

"This has always been called the 'Eastern Room'," the Marquis explained, "and I thought your pictures and mine would feel at home here."

He smiled at her and as she met his eyes he said:

"You look even lovelier than you did last night! How could you disappear in that ridiculous manner when you knew how much I wanted to talk to you?"

"Y.You . . frighten me!"

"Frighten you?"

It was obviously an explanation the Marquis had not expected.

"Please," Ilita said, "I have been . . thinking over what happened, and although it was so . . wonderful . . the most wonderful thing that ever . . happened to me . . you must not kiss me again."

"Why not?" the Marquis asked.

"Because . . if you do I shall have to . . leave here . . and as I have already told you . . I have . . nowhere else to go."

"Do you think I would let you leave?" the Marquis asked. "How could I do without you? And how could Her Ladyship, for that matter, manage if you were not here?"

"I want to stay," Ilita said. "I want desperately to stay . . but . . please . . you know it is wrong of you to . . kiss me . . and it would be . . impossible for the servants not to be aware of what was . . happening unless we behave . . formally as we . . should do."

"Are you really saying that you expect me to treat you as if you were just a reader to my stepmother," the Marquis asked, "knowing what we feel about each other?"

"Please . . try to understand," Ilita pleaded.

"I am trying," he replied, "but it would make it very much easier if you would tell me what you are hiding, and why you are afraid of the love which I can see in your eyes and which I felt on your lips."

"No . . no!" Ilita said. "I cannot do that! Please do not press me into telling you what I must . . tell no one."

The Marquis stood looking at her as she spoke. Then he said:

"You are making it very difficult for me to know what to do. Oh, my dear, do you not understand? I have fallen in love with you as I never thought possible to love anyone; least of all a person I had only just met, and about whom I know nothing."

"That is what you must keep remembering," Ilita said in a low voice, "that you know nothing about me, and it is therefore quite impossible for you to love me as you . . think you do."

"I *do* love you!" the Marquis insisted. "I love you with all my heart, and that is the truth!"

There was silence. Then he said:

"I know you love me! No one's lips could be so soft, sweet and innocent, and I knew when I kissed you that you gave me your heart. That is true, is it not?"

"Y.yes . . that is true," Ilita whispered in a hesitating little voice, "but still . . I cannot tell you my secret . . and I am so desperately afraid that I cannot stay . . here with you . . as I want to do."

"And I want you to," the Marquis said. "Be brave enough to be honest with me! Be courageous and trust me! You know I will never betray your trust or hurt you in any way."

"This is the sort of thing I was afraid you would say," Ilita whispered. "That is why I tried to keep out of your way. I only came downstairs because I thought you would not return so early."

"I came back because I had to be near you," the Marquis said. "I have thought about you all day, although it seems impossible."

He gave a deep sigh.

"I imagined that nothing could be more important than repairing the damage that has been done ever since I have been away, giving orders for the farms to be restored, the stable roofs to be mended, the old servants who had been thrown out to be reinstated. And yet all the time I found myself thinking of you, seeing your face in front of my eyes. Feeling your lips beneath mine!"

There was a note of passion in his voice which made Ilita's heart turn over in her breast.

The Marquis drew a little nearer and his voice was very low and beguiling as he said:

"Tell me, darling, what are you hiding from me? Tell me. However difficult your problem may be, let us share it together."

"That is . . what I want," Ilita said miserably, "but I . . cannot . . cannot tell you what you . . want to know."

There was a little break in her voice which told the Marquis she was not far from tears.

Then because he was an intelligent man and experienced in the ways of women, he started to talk of the pictures of the desert and despite herself, Ilita's agitation left her.

She found herself enthralled by the story of how, when he had read his father's will he had gone to London in despair, thinking that if he stayed and saw his stepmother it would be difficult not to throttle her with his bare hands, knowing that she had tricked his father when he was ill and not in his right senses.

Had he been himself, his father would have known it to be impossible to keep up the house and the estate without more money, and the Marquis was certain in his own mind that it was all a plot thought up by his stepmother who had never liked him.

It was obvious, therefore, that his father had signed a codicil to his will having no idea what he was doing.

But this was something he could not prove, and he felt obliged to leave the Castle immediately after his father's funeral.

He had gone to London wondering whether he should consult Solicitors and fight a law suit against his stepmother, or merely accept the situation and find something else to do which would not involve the handling of his estate.

It was of course his in name, but with no money he knew he would not have any authority.

It was then at his Club that he had met an old friend who told him he was leaving in two days for Africa.

"We are going to do some big game shooting," he said, "and explore parts of the desert and of the Rif Mountains which have not been explored before. I also intend to make some drawings to add to my collection of pictures which I appreciate, if no one else does!"

The Marquis remembered his friend was in fact a very talented artist, though he refused to paint or draw anything that was conventional or what the critics admired.

He had his own method of using paints and crayons, and although the Marquis admired what he did enormously, most critics were very scathing and considered his ideas were far too advanced and outrageous to be considered seriously.

It had not been difficult for the Marquis to agree to join his friend, and they set out two days later, the Marquis thinking of what he had left behind with a bitterness and anger which gradually became a little less pronounced the further he travelled from England.

On his return a year later he knew that however incensed he was by what had happened, he had to see his home and find out what was going on there.

It was then, having arrived unexpectedly at the Castle, that he found Ilita and her luggage on the steps.

"You frightened me," she said when he got to that part of the story.

"I could not understand what was happening," the Marquis explained. "When I left home there were footmen always in the hall ready to open the door immediately. If somebody arrived, whether they were expected or not, there was always a red carpet laid down on the steps."

He laughed.

"You looked very strange, my darling, with all your

117

trunks around you and your eyes large and frightened under your bonnet."

Now they were back to talking about themselves and Ilita knew it was a mistake and she should go to bed.

"I am tired," she said, "it had been a long day, but I have never known your stepmother so happy."

"Pray Heaven she will marry Grantham, and we shall not have to worry about her," the Marquis said.

"If she could see, she wants to live in the Dower House," Ilita remarked. "She thinks it is very attractive."

"That is true," the Marquis agreed. "I will show it to you tomorrow, and you will see it is one of the loveliest houses on the estate, with a garden which has not been changed since it was laid by my ancestor while her husband was at the wars with Marlborough.

"I would love to see it," Ilita said, then remembered that if she was sensible she would not go with the Marquis to see the Dower House, or anywhere else.

She rose to her feet and reluctantly he rose too.

"I will take you upstairs."

"I can manage quite well on my own."

"I want to look after you," he said in a low voice. "I want to protect you, but you make things very difficult for me."

They walked up the stairs side by side.

Then when she thought the Marquis would leave her as his bedroom was in another direction, he came with her towards her own room and she had the frightening idea that he might be intending to kiss her goodnight.

She knew in fact that every nerve in her body was longing for it, but she knew too that it was something that must not happen.

Then as she reached her room she stopped, determined to go no further, and heard a scream.

Without any doubt it came from the Marchioness's room and Ilita ran across the corridor and opened the door of the bedroom to stand transfixed by what she saw.

The candles were lit on the dressing table and standing

near it were two people, one she recognised as Jones, the lady's-maid, and the other was a man.

Even as she stood looking at them the Marchioness gave another scream crying:

"You shall not have my jewels – I will not let you take them away from me!"

The Marquis came into the room behind Ilita to demand:

"What the devil are you doing here, Sheldon?"

The man called Sheldon turned round as the Marquis spoke and Ilita drew in her breath as she saw he held a revolver in his hand.

He pointed it at the Marquis saying:

"You're not goin' to stop me, M'Lord. You turned me out without a reference, and I've got to think of my future!"

"Do not be a fool, Sheldon!" the Marquis retorted. "If you steal Her Ladyship's jewels you will be caught and receive a long term in prison."

"Don't you pay no attention to him!" Jones screamed. "We've got to think of ourselves and get out of the country before he can stop us. Shoot him! Shoot him in the leg! No one'll hear in this part of the house!"

She spoke shrilly, her words tumbling over themselves.

Then as the Marquis was still beside her, and Ilita knew he was calculating how he could disarm his ex-secretary and at the same time avoid being shot in the process, the Marchioness unexpectedly flung herself from the bed and clung with both hands on to Sheldon's arm.

He was taken by surprise and raised the revolver to bring it down sharply on her head, knocking her on to the floor.

As he did so the Marquis sprang forward, giving him a swift upper-cut to the jaw which knocked him backwards so that he fell with a crash against the dressing table, upsetting a number of things that were on it including the candlesticks.

At the same time, as he slithered to the floor only

half-conscious, the maid Jones screamed hysterically.

The Marquis took the revolver from Sheldon's hand as he tried to pull him into a sitting position.

Ilita meanwhile rushed to the side of the bed where the Marchioness was lying with her eyes closed.

She tried to lift her, folding her arms around her and cradling her as if she was a child.

Jones's ministrations had caused Sheldon to open his eyes and he looked up at the Marquis standing over him.

"Now listen to me," the Marquis said, "I will give you two a chance to get out of here, off my estate. If I ever see you again I will have you arrested for attempted murder and theft! Is that clear?"

Sheldon only groaned his acknowledgement as, with Jones pulling him, he managed to struggle to his feet.

The Marquis was aware he had been drinking, but he was sober enough to keep a wary eye on the revolver which was now pointing at him.

"Get out," the Marquis ordered, "and think yourself fortunate that I am being lenient with you!"

There was nothing further the two malefactors could say, and limping, with Jones supporting him, Sheldon walked towards the door. He did not look back before he left the bedroom.

Only when he was quite certain they had gone did the Marquis put the revolver down on the dressing table and turn towards his stepmother.

He realised that the Marchioness was only semi-conscious from the blow she had received, and bending down he picked her up in his arms and laid her on the bed.

"Is there any brandy?" he asked Ilita.

"I think there is some in a decanter in the *Boudoir*," she answered.

She ran across the room and opened the door into the *Boudoir*.

Fortunately the tray on which she had seen the brandy was not far from the doorway, and by the light of the candles in the bedroom she was able to pick up the small decanter which she hoped was brandy and carrying it and a wine glass she hurried back to the Marquis.

He poured out a teaspoonful or so into a glass and held it to his stepmother's lips.

He knew as he did so that she was coming back to consciousness and he said quietly:

"It is all right. There is nothing now to frighten you. Just drink this."

He placed the glass against her lips and after a moment she took a small sip.

"More!" he ordered. "It will make you feel better!"

She was too weak to protest but she shuddered as the fiery liquid went down her throat.

Gently he put her head back against the pillows.

Ilita ran round to the other side of the bed to hold her hand reassuringly, and push back the dark hair from her oval forehead.

She might be dazed and half-conscious, but she still looked exceedingly beautiful.

Then she asked, and it was difficult to mouth the words:

"Have they – stolen – my jewels?"

"They have taken nothing," the Marquis said, "and I promise you they will not come back. I am sorry this should have happened."

"Does your head hurt very much?" Ilita asked.

"I am – all right," the Marchioness said hesitatingly.

Then suddenly she gave a cry which made Ilita jump.

"I can see!" she exclaimed. "I can see your face! I – can – see!"

Chapter Seven

Ilita woke with a feeling she had overslept, and when she saw the time by the clock beside her bed she gave a little cry of horror.

She rang the bell and when the maid came in she said quickly:

"Is Her Ladyship awake? I am afraid I am very late!"

"It's all right, Miss," the maid said. "Her Ladyship hasn't stirred. I peeped in once or twice but she was sleeping like a child, so there's no need for you to worry."

Ilita gave a little sigh of relief and lay back against her pillows.

It had been after three o'clock when they had finally gone to bed, unable to stop talking after the excitement of finding the Marchioness could see.

At first she was aware only of the lights and anything that was very near to her, as she had seen Ilita's face.

Then gradually she kept exclaiming as other parts of the room came into focus.

"You must not tire yourself and do too much too quickly!" Ilita warned.

But it was impossible for them all not to feel elated and thrilled at what had occured.

The Marquis said it must have been the blow on her head which brought back her sight, just as it had been a blow when she fell from her horse that had taken it away from her.

"I do not mind how it happened!" the Marchioness exclaimed. "In fact I am willing to give Sheldon all my jewels to thank him for having been instrumental in giving me my sight back."

"He certainly does not deserve that!" the Marquis said

sharply. "I only let them go so that there might be no scandal. I knew you would not wish to be questioned about what happened."

The Marchioness shivered.

"No, of course not! And if I had still been blind I would have refused to say anything."

"I do not want you to say anything now!" the Marquis said. "The best possible thing is for us to keep it secret amongst ourselves. If the servants get to know what has happened, sooner or later somebody outside the castle will talk, and it will be in the newspapers."

"That is certainly something to be prevented!" the Marchioness agreed.

The Marquis insisted on their having a glass of champagne which he fetched from downstairs, and he and Ilita sat on the Marchioness's bed, toasting her and wishing her happiness.

She looked so lovely, with her face radiant, her large dark eyes continually wandering about the room to be quite certain she could see everything.

Ilita felt in a way it was sad that Lord Grantham could not be there to see her.

As if what she was thinking communicated itself to the Marquis he said:

"One person you can tell what has happened is Grantham. He will understand. At the same time I am sure he would not wish you to talk about it to anyone else."

"Of course not," the Marchioness agreed.

Then as Ilita took her empty glass from her she put her hand over hers and said:

"I am sure, dearest child, this is all due to you! If you had not made me think differently about everything and given me hope, I think by this time I would have killed myself from sheer depression."

"You are not to say such things!" Ilita said. "Everything has changed now, and you must forget the past."

"I am sure you are right," the Marquis agreed.

"I am quite certain," Ilita went on, "that you must rest

your eyes and try to go to sleep. There will be so much to see in the morning, and you must explain to Mrs. Lynton that when you first opened your eyes you could see the sun coming through the sides of the curtains."

"I *shall* see it! I shall really see it!" the Marchioness said in a rapt tone.

Then she held out her hand to the Marquis to say goodnight. To Ilita's delight and surprise, and perhaps his too, he bent and kissed her cheek.

"It was very brave of you to tackle Sheldon," he said, "and thank you for giving me back the estate. The first thing I am going to do is to put the Dower House in order."

The Marchioness smiled and her fingers tightened on his.

"I feel" she said softly, "that it has been waiting for me for a very long time!"

When Ilita got into bed she said a fervent prayer of thankfulness that everything had come right, not only for the Marchioness but also for the Marquis.

At the same time her own problem remained unsolved and now that she was awake it was back in her mind, and once again she was wondering how she could prevent herself from telling the Marquis who she was.

She was so afraid of the disastrous consequence that she thought she must be resolute and resist him, however much he pleaded with her.

But she loved him so fervently that she knew it would be difficult not to obey him in anything he demanded of her.

The door of her room opened and the maid came in carrying a breakfast tray.

"I thought, Miss, you must be as tired as Her Ladyship is," she said, "so I've brought you your breakfast in bed."

"How kind of you!" Ilita exclaimed. "You are making me feel spoiled and very indolent, Emily."

"Well, you wants someone to look after you," Emily said. "They've all been saying downstairs as no one could

124

have done more for Her Ladyship than you have. It's a real pleasure to see the whole Castle looking as it used to, and the floors are that clean that you could eat your food off them!"

Ilita laughed, but she knew that everybody in the house thought it was due to her influence over the Marchioness that the Marquis's authority had been restored.

As her mother had said, you could not keep anything secret from the servants, and because all of them had been in the castle for so long they thought of it as theirs, and were personally involved in everything that happened.

When Emily put the breakfast tray down beside her bed Ilita saw there was a note on it and her heart leapt as she was sure she recognised the handwriting.

As soon as Emily had left the room she tore open the envelope and found she was right. It was from the Marquis, and he had written:

"I have to go to London very early, but I hope to be back either late tonight or first thing tomorrow morning. Take care of yourself.

                              L."

Ilita read it and re-read it, and although there was nothing very intimate in what the Marquis had written she felt as if his vibrations leapt out from the writing paper towards her and it was almost as if he kissed her.

"I love him!" she told herself. "But it is something I should not do!"

She felt it was impossible for her to feel unhappy after all that had happened, and she was not surprised when half-an-hour later Emily burst into the room to cry excitedly:

"Mrs. Lynton says to come at once, Miss! She's with her Ladyship and a miracle's happened. Her Ladyship can see!"

Ilita managed to express surprise, and when she went to the Marchioness's room it was to find Mrs. Lynton and several housemaids all grouped round the bed.

They were listening with obvious joy as the Marchioness told them that when she had woken up she had been able to see the sunshine.

"I know you will be pleased, Miss Marsh," she said.

"I can only thank God that all our prayers have been answered," Ilita replied quietly.

She would not allow the Marchioness to exert herself too early, although she was so excited that she wanted to get up and go downstairs without being helped and walk in the garden.

Ilita suggested she send a note to Lord Grantham with a groom inviting him to luncheon.

For a moment the Marchioness stared at her. Then she said:

"That is something else I can now do! Eat with those I love instead of fumbling alone in the dark."

"Everything will be as it used to be," Ilita said, "but I think you ought to see the Eye Specialist in case he has any suggestions to make."

"I would rather have yours," the Marchioness said. "That my eyes feel quite strong is due to the vegetables you have made me eat, and of course the honey in which you believe."

"I wish my mother could hear you say that!" Ilita replied. "She always believed that the right food is more important than any medicine."

She was about to tell the Marchioness of how her mother had persuaded many of the Arab women to feed their children the right way, then remembered that she was Miss Marsh, who had always lived in the English countryside.

'It is difficult to keep remembering that,' she thought, and later in the day when she had a moment to herself she went to the Eastern Room to look at the pictures of the desert.

That gave her the idea that she felt closer not only to her father but also the the Marquis.

When finally she left the room to go back upstairs she

was longing for him so intensely that it was a physical pain.

*   *   *

The Marquis, having arrived in London, went first to his Club for luncheon, then because he had time before he called, as he intended, on the Countess of Darrington, he went to Tattersall's.

There was a sale taking place the next day and he left bids on three horses which he intended to be the beginning of the new stables he would build at the Castle.

As he gave his name he found himself thinking that it was all due to Ilita that he was able to anticipate spending so much money.

It all seemed incredible that one very young girl could have changed his whole life as she had changed that of his stepmother.

He had a strange desire to be with her, but he had come to London for a special reason which he knew was extremely important to both of them.

After sacking Sheldon he had looked through the contents of his desk in the office and found, amongst a miscellaneous collection of bills, the letter the Countess of Darrington had written to his stepmother suggesting she should have a reader.

She had been very glowing in her praise for a Miss Marsh whom she said she had employed, and as soon as he read it the Marquis had known this was the clue he needed to find out why Ilita was so frightened, and why she would not confide in him.

It was just about four o'clock, which he knew was the social time for calling, when he arrived at Darrington House.

The front door was open, there were footmen in the hall, and as one of them took his hat and directed him upstairs without asking his name, the Marquis was aware, although it was not what he had expected, that the Countess was having an 'at home' day.

He was well aware that it was customary amongst the

Ladies of Society to have one afternoon a week when their houses were open to their friends to have tea in the State Drawing Room.

They had no idea whether they would be receiving a hundred or only a dozen guests, but everyone was welcome.

Slowly the Marquis went up the stairs and as he entered the big double Drawing-Room he realised he had arrived early.

At a quick glance it was obvious there was no one in the room.

He was walking to where there was an arrangement of hot-house flowers narrowing the opening between the two rooms, when he heard voices.

He realised his hostess must be receiving in a further room and moved on without hurrying over the Aubusson carpet, pausing for a moment to appreciate a very fine picture by Canaletto which would have matched the two he possessed at the castle.

Then he heard a man say angrily:

"Surely you should have been informed of this before it got into the newspapers?"

"The man called yesterday, and I recall now that he sounded if he might be a Solicitor, but I sent a message to say I was busy and would see him tomorrow."

"That was certainly a mistake! He may get in touch with the girl."

"There is no likelihood of that, for no one but you and I know that she is at Lyss Castle."

The Marquis, who had just been about to walk into the next room, froze.

"Well, there is certainly something you will have to do about this," the man said, "and it was a mistake to send her away."

"How was I to guess? How was I to imagine for one moment," the woman answered, who the Marquis was sure was the Countess of Darrington, "that her god-mother, a tiresome interfering woman I always thought,

128

would have left her an enormous fortune?"

"The newspapers say it runs into millions!"

The Countess laughed.

"Then we will certainly help Ilita to spend it."

"There will be plenty of people only too ready to do that," the man to whom she was speaking replied. "The whole Darrington-Coombe family will come swarming in like bees round a honey-pot!"

"Of course they will," the Countess replied, "but I am her guardian until Anthony comes of age which will be seven years from now, and a lot can happen in that time."

"And a guardian has complete control over his or her ward!" the man said slowly as if he was thinking it out.

"Of course!" the Countess agreed. "And I made it very clear to Ilita when I sent her away that she was to do as I had arranged, or she would be very, very sorry."

"What did you threaten her with?"

"Being incarcerated in a Convent."

"Good God! It is fortunate in the circumstances you did nothing of the sort!"

"Stop frightening me!" the Countess said plaintively. "The girl is now employed by the Marchioness of Lyss. And since she is blind it is unlikely that she will see the newspapers before we get there tomorrow to bring her back here."

"I suppose you are right," the man said doubtfully. "No wait!"

He made a sudden sound that was almost a cry.

"What is it, Paul?" the Countess asked.

"I have an idea! It is a stupendous one! You must not bring her back here with the family telling her how important she is."

"Then what are you suggesting?"

"That I marry her!"

"Marry her?"

The Countess's voice was incredulous.

"I will get a Special Licence," Paul said, as if he was thinking aloud. "We will then go to the Castle and the moment you arrive you will order her, as her guardian, to marry me. Once she is my wife there is nothing anybody can do about it!"

"But Paul, my dear . ."

"Do not distress yourself, it will make no difference to you and me. Even though you love me, you have always said you have no wish to give up your title to marry an obscure and impecunious Baronet. I am, however, sure this will make all the difference. We will have money – unlimited money to do what we wish, go where we want to. A wife can always be left behind to look after the children."

There was silence for a moment, then the Countess said doubtfully:

"You really think that is the sensible thing to do?"

"Of course it is," Paul answered, "and all our difficulties, yours and mine, will be solved. Money means power, money means having exactly what you want, being able to go anywhere in the world that takes one's fancy."

The Countess gave a deep sigh.

"I suppose you are right."

"Of course I am right. Now do not worry your head about it. Just leave everything to me. I will get a Special Licence as soon as the Office in the Law Courts is open tomorrow morning. After that, when you are ready, we will head for Lyss."

"It seems a crazy idea," the Countess said in a low voice, "but, I suppose, a practical one."

"Very practical and very enjoyable," Paul said. "Now let us hide this newspaper, and let us hope that none of your guests this afternoon will have read it."

The Marquis did not wait to hear any more.

Quietly and swiftly he retraced his steps and crossed the empty Drawing-Room to hurry down the stairs.

He took his hat from the attendant footman and went out into the afternoon sunshine.

As he glanced at his watch he realised that it was too

late to do what he wanted and he would have to wait until the next morning.

But the first thing was to find a newsagent's and buy today's newspapers.

*   *   *

Ilita felt that the sunshine coming in through the windows of the Eastern Room was more golden than it had ever been and had a particular radiance about it.

She knew this was because in two hours, perhaps earlier, the Marquis would be back and she would see him.

She had hoped fervently he would return the night before, but when he had not done so she had gone to bed to dream of him and awake with an irrepressible feeling of happiness.

On a table in front of her was a basket filled with flowers which the gardeners had brought in from the greenhouses, and as she came downstairs, while the Marchioness was having her bath, she had found them setting out an elaborate arrangement in the Drawing-Room.

She complimented them on how beautiful they had made the house ever since the Marquis's return, and told them it must be even more beautiful today when the Marchioness would be able to see how lovely the flowers were.

She had chosen from the huge bunches of flowers they had with them the ones she wanted to arrange herself in the Eastern Room.

These included several varieties of white and coloured lilies, and also a number of orchids.

These were specially appropriate to the pictures of the desert and the others depicting wild animals.

One of the varieties of orchids she had chosen consisted of small white star-shaped flowers with a dozen or more blooms on a single stem.

As she held them in her hand she could not help thinking how perfect they looked against the new gown she was wearing for the first time.

The seamstress had now finished it, and when Ilita

looked at herself in the mirror she thought she looked very different from the way she had appeared in her out-grown schoolgirl clothes, and wondered if the Marquis would notice.

She felt sure he would, and even to think of him appreciating her brought a flush of colour to her cheeks.

She was looking down at the orchids in her hand when the door opened and as she turned her head casually, thinking it was one of the servants, she gave a cry of delight.

It was the Marquis who stood there, looking exceedingly smart in his driving-clothes.

He was back far earlier than she had dared to expect.

"You are back! You are back!" she cried, because she was so pleased to see him.

He shut the door behind him, and as he came towards her she thought there was a strange expression on his face she did not understand.

She also noticed that he carried a newspaper in his hand.

"I want to speak to you, Ilita!"

"I expect you want to hear that Her Ladyship is very well and we are certain that her sight is now as perfect as it ever was!"

"I am not interested for the moment in my stepmother, but in you!"

Ilita looked at him. Then she gave a little cry.

"What has happened? What is wrong?"

"There is nothing wrong, at least I do not think you will think so, but I want you to read this."

He held out the newspaper as he spoke and Ilita took it from him in surprise.

She saw it was folded over the centre page and she read:

"HUGE AMERICAN FORTUNE FOR PEER'S DAUGHTER.

"It has just been learned that Mrs. Grace Van Holden, widow of the Texan multi-millionaire who died last month, has left her entire fortune of several million

pounds sterling to her God-daughter, Lady Ilita Darrington-Coombe.

Mrs. Van Holden was, before her marriage, the daughter of Lord Downshire, and Lady Ilita is the only child of the late 5th Earl of Darrington who died abroad last year.

It is believed that Lady Ilita is now in England and the Van Holden Solicitors are trying to contact her."

The Marquis's eyes were on Ilita's face as she read what was in the newspaper.

Then she looked up at him to say:

"H.how did you . . know this was . . me?"

The Marquis reached out and took the newspaper from her, and taking her hands in his he said quietly:

"Listen, Ilita. I went yesterday to call on your aunt because I had discovered it was she who had recommended you as a reader. I wanted to find out if I could why you were so frightened, and what this secret was you were hiding from me."

Ilita made an inarticulate little sound and her eyes fell before his, but she did not speak and he went on:

"While I was at Darrington House I overheard a man tell your aunt what you have just read in the newspaper. They plan to come here today with a Special Licence and, as your aunt is your guardian, whom you have to obey, she will force you to marry this man."

For a moment Ilita could only stare at the Marquis and her eyes seemed to fill her whole face. Then she gave a little scream of terror.

"Hide me!" she begged frantically. "Please . . hide me so that Aunt Sybil cannot . . find me!"

She would have run away as if to find somewhere to hide herself if the Marquis had not held her hands firmly in his.

Then he said, still very quietly:

"I have a better idea than that and one which will ensure you will be safe for ever."

"What . . is it?"

Ilita could hardly say the words because her lips were trembling.

"It is that you should be married," the Marquis said, "but to me!"

There was a silence that made it seem as if no one breathed.

Then Ilita said in a whisper so that he could hardly hear:

"Did you . . say I should . . marry you?"

"I love you!" the Marquis said. "I had wanted before all this happened to ask you to be my wife, but I had a feeling that because you were so secretive you might refuse me unless I knew what was keeping us apart. Now I know who you are, and there is nothing to stop us from being married. But it must be quickly, my darling, before your aunt and this man whom she favours as your husband arrive."

Ilita gave a little scream that she could not suppress.

"Aunt Sybil will . . make me do what she . . wants," she said, "or she will put me into a Convent."

"She will not do that at the moment," the Marquis said grimly, "not while she has the chance of getting her hands on your fortune. But it would make things very simple if when they arrive it is to find you already have a husband to protect and look after you, which is what I want to do."

Ilita held on to his hand as if certain that if he was not there to sustain her she might fall down. Then she said:

"Please . . I want to be . . with you."

For the first time the Marquis smiled and it seemed to illuminate his whole face.

"That is what I want, my precious," he said, "more than I have ever wanted anything in my whole life. Come, everything is arranged."

"You mean . . just as I . . am?" Ilita said vaguely.

The Marquis looked at her and drew in his breath.

"I will tell you later how beautiful you are, but now let us not waste time."

Then as he saw the flowers on the table his eyes were

twinkling and he picked up a spray of orchids.

"Put these in your hair, my sweet," he said. "They will make you a bridal wreath, for we have no time to look for one."

As Ilita obeyed him, securing the orchids to the back of her head with two hairpins, the Marquis selected several of the exotic lilies she had brought to the Eastern Room because she thought they were appropriate and placed them in her arms.

They were white with yellow stamens and a very rare species that the late Marquis had brought to England from Burma.

The Marquis looked down at her and she thought for a moment that he was going to kiss her, but he only said:

"I love you, and when you are my wife I will tell you how much!"

Then swiftly he opened the door and hurried Ilita along the passage to the hall.

At the foot of the steps his Chaise was waiting, and as he helped Ilita into it the groom, who was holding the horses' heads, ran to jump up behind.

Then the Marquis was driving swiftly towards the Church which stood just outside the gates opposite the village green.

It was an old Church that had been built in the reign of Queen Elizabeth and had remained unaltered over the ages.

Nearly every member of the Lyss family had been buried there, and the Church itself was filled with exquisitely carved memorials to those who had died in battle or occupied some important position of State.

The Marquis drew up his horse and jumped down to lift Ilita to the ground. She could hear the music of the organ playing inside the Church and saw as she entered that the old Parson was standing in front of the altar waiting for them.

There was nobody else except the organist in the Church, and yet as Ilita heard the Marquis say his marriage vows in a strong, resonant voice and she heard her own voice answering very softly, she felt as if not only the Marquis's mother was watching her son being married to somebody he loved, but her own father and mother were also there.

They were telling her that they had heard her cries for help and she need never be afraid that they would not love and protect her.

'I am so lucky . . so very, very lucky,' Ilita thought.

As she held tightly on to the Marquis's hand and the Parson blessed them, she felt her whole being rise in a paean of thankfulness that she had found not only the security she had always longed for but also the love that was part of God.

Having signed the Marriage Register they walked together from the Church to the triumphant sound of Handel's Wedding March out into the sunshine.

Only as he helped her back into the Chaise did she feel the Marquis relax and was aware that he had been afraid that he might not be able to save her from her aunt and the man who wanted her fortune.

Slowly, because now there was no hurry, they drove back under the great oak trees to where the sunshine on the windows of the great house told them it was waiting for them.

"Is it . . true . . is it really . . true . . that I am your . . wife?" Ilita whispered.

"You are mine, my darling," the Marquis replied.

She gave a little sigh of happiness. Then she said:

"Suppose you had not gone to London? Suppose they had arrived and I had no idea why?"

"Do not think about it," the Marquis said in his deep voice. "You are safe and no one shall ever hurt you again. I swear I will kill anyone who makes you as frightened as you were when I first saw you."

They arrived back at the castle to find that the red carpet had already been rolled down the steps.

Then as the Marquis and Ilita walked into the hall and saw Glover waiting for them he said:

"I want you to be the first to know, Glover, since you have been here longer at the Castle than anybody else, that I am married and my wife and I both hope that you will wish us every happiness!"

For a moment Glover could only gasp. Then he said:

"That is good news! Very good news indeed, M'Lord, and on behalf of myself and the staff may I hope you will have many years together!"

After that it seemed to Ilita that she heard nothing but cries of astonishment and delight that she and the Marquis were married.

"Why did you not tell me what you were going to do?" the Marchioness demanded. "You know how much I would have liked to attend the ceremony!"

Quietly her stepson explained to her who Ilita really was, the way in which her aunt had behaved towards her in the past, and what she had intended for her in the future.

"It is monstrous!" the Marchioness exclaimed. "I have never heard such a thing! To be truthful I have always disliked Sybil Darrington because I thought she was jealous of me. I was therefore exceedingly surprised when she wrote me such a kind letter suggesting I might need a reader."

"I want to thank you for agreeing to have me," Ilita said. "Supposing you had refused? Anything might have happened to me!"

She shivered as she spoke and the Marquis knew she was thinking her aunt might have sent her into a Convent as she had threatened to do.

"It is all over," he said.

At that moment Glover appeared in the doorway to say:

"The Countess of Darrington is downstairs, M'Lord, and with her is Mr. Paul Perceval. They asked to see Her Ladyship, but when I told them you were in residence they asked to speak to you first."

At Glover's words Ilita went very pale and reached out

her hand to the Marquis as though she must cling on to him for safety.

"I will deal with this!" he said firmly. "Stay here and do not worry. There is nothing they can do but return to London where I am going to send them as quickly as possible!"

There was a grim note in his voice which told Ilita how deeply he resented the way she had been treated, and because she knew he could be very frightening when he was angry, she was glad that she was not in her aunt's place.

At the same time it was almost impossible to believe that all her fears were now unnecessary and she was the Marquis's wife.

"You are not to worry," the Marchioness said, who was watching the expression on her face. "Instead we will talk about me, and how soon I can move into the Dower House. I am quite aware that you and Terill will not want me here now."

"We would not want you to think we are turning you out," Ilita said quickly.

"I want to be turned out," the Marchioness said. "I want to marry Gerald, and I want to forget all the misery of the past nine months and also the years when I was not really happy, although he was very kind, married to Terill's father."

"You were too young for him," Ilita said softly.

"Of course I was, and it was a great mistake to be carried away by the glitter and the glamour of being a Marchioness, instead of waiting until I had found somebody I could love."

Then she gave a little laugh.

"And yet Fate moves in a strange and unexpected manner. If I had married Gerald when I was young we should have been very poor and perhaps not as happy as we shall be now when I have enough money of my own for us to be extremely comfortable and do everything we want to do."

"You are right. Fate is very strange," Ilita said. "If I

had not come back to England because there was no more money to pay for my schooling at the Convent, Aunt Sybil would never have wished to get rid of me by sending me to you as your reader."

"It is all complex and twisted, but at the same time very exciting!" the Marchioness said. "And now, my dearest child, the most important thing for both of us to do is to plan our *trousseaux*."

Ilita gave a little laugh that seemed like the song of the birds outside.

"I never thought about it until now," she said. "All I have to wear are two gowns made from some muslin that was intended for curtains, and I cannot believe His Lordship will find me very alluring in those!"

"I do not think that will worry him," the Marchioness said wisely. "At the same time, I am going to send to London immediately for the best dressmakers in Bond Street to bring us tomorrow all the gowns they have ready and the material and sketches for a great many more!"

It sounded so entrancing that Ilita forgot for the moment, at any rate, what was happening downstairs.

When the Marquis came back into the *Boudoir* she gave a little cry and ran towards him, holding on to him frantically in case something had gone wrong.

"It is all right, my precious," he said tenderly. "They have left and it is doubtful if you will ever see your aunt again."

"Was she very angry?" Ilita questioned.

"She was more stunned and astonished that you should be married, and although she tried to bluster that it was without her permission and therefore illegal, she knew there was really nothing she could do. Trying to make trouble would only make her a laughing-stock."

The Marquis's eyes twinkled and he was still smiling as he said:

"Not even the most critical guardian could pretend that you had not made a marriage of consequence as far as the Social World is concerned."

Ilita put her face against his shoulder.

"It would not . . matter to me . . who you were."

"I know that," the Marquis said, "and now, my darling, I am going to take you away so that we can talk about ourselves, and there is a visitor waiting impatiently to take our place."

There was no need to say this was Lord Grantham, and as he came into the *Boudoir* the Marquis and Ilita left.

He took her downstairs and they went instinctively to the Eastern Room as if they both knew it was waiting for them.

In their absence the flowers Ilita had left in the basket had all been arranged in vases, and the sunshine coming in through the windows seemed to illuminate in a very special way the pictures of the desert.

The Marquis put his arms round Ilita as they stood in front of the pictures and said:

"One day I will take you back and we will look at the Falls together, but first we must spend a little while here at the Castle so that I can put in hand everything that needs doing. Then, my darling, I am taking you to Devonshire where I have a house in which I used to stay as a boy. It is very quiet, and we can be alone there and get to know each other a little better than we do at the moment."

"I feel I have known you for . . a thousand years," Ilita whispered, "perhaps even longer than that."

"That is what I feel about you," the Marquis said. "At the same time, we have to catch up with the years in between when we were searching for each other and thought we would never meet."

His arms tightened as he said:

"Suppose I had never found you? Suppose I had never realised that I could feel like this, or that love could be such an amazing experience that there are no words in which to describe it?"

Ilita threw back her head to look up at him.

"I love you! I . . love you! And I know that Papa was guiding me towards you and that it was our Fate . . our

Karma . . that we should meet . . and nothing could have prevented us from . . finding each other."

The Marquis did not answer.

He was kissing her wildly, passionately, demandingly, as if he was still afraid that he might lose her and he wanted to make sure she was his.

*　　　*　　　*

Later that night in the huge, gilt-carved canopied bed in which all the previous Marchionesses of Lyss had started their married life, Ilita move a little closer to her husband and whispered:

"I . . know now that the Castle is . . enchanted!"

"It lost its enchantment for a brief while," the Marquis said, "but you, darling, with your special magic have brought it back to what I believed it to be when I was a child, and what it had meant to many generations who have lived here and been supremely happy."

"That is what we must make it for everybody," Ilita said. "I thought today, when Mrs. Lynton was crying because we were married, and Glover looked years younger because he was so pleased, that because we are so wonderfully happy, it will radiate out to everybody we meet."

"I am sure it will," the Marquis said, "and there is so much for us to do, my precious, not only here, but on the other estates I own in different parts of England, to encourage the young people to seek prosperity and to make sure that we are developing everything on sensible and modern lines which will mean we can employ many more people than we do at the moment."

"That is what I would like to do," Ilita said, "and . . please . . please . . let me help you. You are so clever, so wise, and I know very little about England because I have never lived here."

"You know more about human beings, and that is more important than anything else," the Marquis said. "It does not matter what nationality people are or what part of the world they come from, they all want

141

happiness, and that is what we will give them."

"And that is what you have . . given me."

He turned so that he could look down at her by the light coming from the flames of a small fire that was burning in the grate, and from the stars outside the window.

The Marquis had pulled back the curtains when they came to bed, and Ilita had exclaimed:

"Now you are making me think of the desert. You know how brilliant the sky looks at night, and how much larger the stars appear than when you look at them here."

"They are the same stars," the Marquis said quietly, "which have drawn you and me together. But my precious little wife, you are my star, and you will lead me and guide me for the rest of my life."

"That is what I want you to think . . and what I want you to say," Ilita answered, "but I am . . so afraid that I may . . fail you."

"How could you do that when you have your perception to guide you? The perception which told you, although not one person in a million would have believed you, that my stepmother would see again!"

"It also told me . . once I had got over being frightened of you . . that you were the most wonderful man in the whole world!"

The Marquis smiled. Then he said:

"It must have been my perception which made me know that you were very different from any other woman I have ever met in my whole life. I could not believe, my lovely one, that you were real, or what you appeared to be."

He laughed very gently as he said:

"How could I have doubted for a moment that you were very young, very innocent, and very, very inexperienced?"

Ilita blushed and hid her face against him.

"Y.you . . will not . . find me . . boring?"

"I find it the most exciting thing that has ever happened to me!" the Marquis said. "I suppose, because I have never known any young girls, that I never expected one to be so unspoilt, so perfect in every way. At the same time so thrilling that I am afraid, my precious, that I may shock you, or make you afraid of me."

"I could never be that," Ilita said, "and . . please . . darling . . just as you are going to teach me to help you with your huge possessions . . teach me to love you as you . . want to be loved . . and make the Castle and everybody in it a Fairy Tale place . . as it seems to be at the moment."

"It will always be like that while you are here," the Marquis said, "and that is what I know one day our children will find."

He felt a little quiver go through Ilita because she was shy and thought that no man could know such happiness or find somebody so unique and different.

"I adore you!" he said. "The only problem is that you may become tired of hearing me say so."

"It is . . what I want to hear," Ilita said, "and every time you say it I feel the words seem to . . thrill through me like little rays of starlight."

The way she spoke with a touch of passion in her voice brought the fire to the Marquis's eyes.

He looked down at her, at her hair falling over the pillow, at her strange eyes looking up into his, and her soft lips trembling a little with excitement.

Then he was kissing her, kissing her demandingly and yet beguilingly, deliberately inciting the little shafts of starlight to grow brighter and turn from the soft silver of the night to the burning fire of the midday sun.

His hands were touching her body, his lips were moving from her mouth to her neck, to her breasts, and Ilita's breath was coming fitfully from between her lips.

"I love you . . oh, Terill . . I . . love you! Please love me . . I want you to love me . .!"

She was not certain whether she said the words aloud, or in her heart.

Then as the Marquis made her his and carried her into the sky, they found the ecstacy and the glory of the love which triumphs over all the difficulties and brings perfection to all those who seek it.